figments,
fragments,
& pigments,

oh my

Carl Grupp

Cover: *Pandora's Bouquet* by Carl Grupp, oil painting.

Scurfpea Publishing
P.O. Box 46
Sioux Falls, SD 57101
scurfpeapublishing.com
editor@scurfpeapublishing.com

figments, fragments, & pigments, oh my

the writings of Carl Grupp

I dedicate this book to my parents, Carl Martin Grupp and Solvieg Marie Grupp, for their love and support.

Contents

Artwork

Knight, Death, and My Devils   *intaglio*

Grupp

Notes from Above Ground

Dear Sir,

    I have been so glad to hear from you that all is well and that your headstone is to your liking and specifications. It certainly seemed quite humorous to all of us at the shop, reading the limerick you wrote for your epithet. It really is a knee-slapper.

    It has been miserably cold here at the outer limits. We are all praying for an early spring. The ground is like granite, so we are constantly having to replace or sharpen broken picks.

    Your new lace wardrobe sounds exquisite. Where on Earth did you find someone to make it? As for me, I can't complain too much, as if it would do me much good if I did. The food is not the best, but there is plenty of it. Last week, some joker dumped a tube of bb's into our morning oatmeal, so that was cause for some excitement and created a brief escape from the usual. A number of people ended up with badly cracked dentures and added to that the misfortune of having bean soup for supper causing a lot of porcelain in the biffys to become badly pitted. So I suppose that they will up the ante, auntie, or whatever, to recoup expenses.

As if this weren't enough, on top of this, some fool made up the asinine rule that we are no longer allowed to use our hands at mealtimes.

You probably recall poor Douglas who lost his right hand four weeks ago in that dreadful powerdrive accident. Well, he suffered another setback attempting to cleanse himself after a bowel movement with that new hook he was fitted with. I guess he will be terribly scarred, thank heavens it won't show. It wouldn't have been so bad if he would have stopped when he first punctured himself, but I guess the poor soul was very embarrassed and had too much pride to call for help. After seventy-two stitches the nurse stopped counting. Stubborn fool, it serves him right. Well try to keep in touch

Truly Yours,

Dear Sir,

Well our prayers have finally been answered and the earth is beginning to thaw. The incessant rain has been a help as well as a hindrance. It is now much easier to dig, but it fills up with water, which in turn causes the walls to crumble. So everything is unstable. Such is life. I have my hopes up about being invited to the Horsemen's Ball next week. Let the chips fall as they may though, I always say. Poor Douglas has had an awful time adapting. I don't know why he didn't get pants with a zipper fly. Well it's just as well he can't have any kids. They would all probably end up as dumb as a mud fence. Can't help but feel sorry for the poor soul though. They are bringing in some sort of therapist La De DA in an attempt to break through to some of us. Fat chance!! There was a woman here admitted last week who had had one of those silicone implants, well Dow Corning, who makes these implants it turns out also make those plastic explosives like we used in Nam. To make a long story short, the shipment got mixed up and her plastic surgeon didn't notice the difference. Well it turns out she was one of those high paid strippers and wouldn't you know it right in the middle of her act where she gets the tassels to go different directions, hear tell she really had them going and it really was spectacular, but she was not used to their new size and weight and she lost her balance and careened around the stage like a drunken Sikorsky helicopter until she bumped into a pole which caused a chain reaction and damned if both her tits didn't explode. The psychological damage has been horrendous.. They say it will be years of therapy to regain one iota of self-esteem. She just quivers and sobs, poor dear. Well nobody can hardly sleep because of her constant wailings. Write when you get work . . . .

Truly Yours,

Grupp

Dear Sir,

The earth is beginning to dry up and that is a blessing as the digging has been going much easier, but as you might imagine, the mosquito population is way out of bounds. I realize that they need sustenance too, but it is getting ridiculous. We are all covered with big red welts. I hope they don't carry any disease.

I made an interesting observation this morning while reading the newspaper. What page of the newspaper is full of pictures of smiling people? You guessed it: the obituaries. You would at least think that some of them would be more than a little pissed off at their demise, especially when so many of them look so young for their age. Perhaps all these smiling faces are trying to tell us that death is not so bad after all.

Poor Douglas did it again . . . this time he was out sunning himself and looked up just in time to have one of those damned pigeons shit right in his eye. He forgot about his prosthesis and took out his right eye and part of his nose. Some people never learn.

I have been attempting to lose weight and to try to get in shape. I try to watch what I eat, but all I seem to see is a blur. Perhaps that is a result of growing up in the Depression. Speaking of depression, I made the mistake of showing a drawing that I did to a friend and he said that it looked like I was in a state of depression when I did it. I said no, I think I was in Iowa.

We are getting ready to let up the kites. It should be glorious. I have constructed an electric kite that will fly without any wind; the problem is it requires unusual lengths of extension cord. I have bought out three hardware stores already. It is certainly worth it though, not to have to rely on those unpredictable thermals anymore.

Truly Yours,

Dear Sir,

Everything has really dried out here now and the earth is again cracked and crumbly. You have to go down at least four feet to find an earthworm, except for a few small retarded ones that don't realize the danger of the heat at the surface. I wish we could learn from those nightcrawler friends of ours. The ground is so hot that you can't stand still in fear of burning your feet. I have sweat out enough liquid to make another one like me. So I needn't have worried about dieting.

For those people who hate to write or at least never have the time to, I am designing postcards with the lettering already done so all people have to do is sign them and send them off to keep in touch. If that is a success, maybe I will branch out into Christmas letters where everyone tells you the highlights of their year. Since the advent of the computer, I have been inundated with these strange beasts of literature. Most of the time everyone seems so happy and in control of their destinies that it makes me want to puke. I'll give them Christmas letters that will cause their gums to bleed and their bladders to burst, not any of this sentimental crap, something that they can serve up with their nasty fruit cakes that nobody can swallow either.

I was in the market for a better car when I had lunch with Vinnie and Doris at that new Chinese restaurant. After sucking the last bits of hot mustard off my chicken bone, I opened my fortune cookie to, I swear to God it's the truth, a fortune that read....THE NEXT CAR YOU BUY WILL BE TROUBLE FREE FOR FORTY THOUSAND MILES.... Well, naturally, I took it as an omen and so purchased the last vehicle I had been looking at. Well, it took thirty days before the clutch went out and the inside door handle fell off, so now I have to open the window to close the door. So much for fortune cookies.

Truly Yours,

Grupp

Dear Sir,

Because of the heat, they have taken us out of the fields and have given us a break. That just seems to make the days last longer, however, so the tedium is great. A couple of my compatriots in boredom found a diversion for an afternoon. One of those cats that are always hanging around caught a mouse and was batting it around; the mouse would think it had escaped when the cat would pounce and bat it around some more. Anyway, Gertie and Frieda stole the mouse away from the cat and tied a cord to its hind leg. Even though the poor thing was dead, they proceeded to tease that cat with it by dragging that mouse back and forth in front of it. Well, much to Gertie and Freida's delight, that old cat eventually ate that mouse. No sooner did that cat get that mouse halfway down, when those girls started to pull on that string to retrieve it. With much retching and wonderful gymnastics on the cat's part, up it came, slippery old mouse. To everyone's joy, that cat must have eaten that mouse thirty times that day before the cord weakened and broke and that poor creature of a cat slunk off, foaming at the mouth. It seems at times like a higher power plays with us as did the girls with the cat, or the cat with the mouse. After that, even the highlights of the day, HA, the week, seemed dreary. That cat will think twice, I bet, before it plays with its food again. . . at least in front of Gertie and Frieda.

There is talk that we might be getting new uniforms, not a moment too soon I say, as mine is in tatters. There

Grupp

is also talk that they might cut down on the medication. I guess all of our incessant drooling is frightening off the customers. Well, keep in touch.

Truly Yours,

Dear Sir,

Well, they had to evacuate the whole camp this afternoon because of a bomb threat. Unfortunately, it was just that, a threat.

The Horseman's Ball was a huge success. I was invited and wore my new uniform which I trimmed up with crocheted collars and hand-sewn epaulets. A little sewing here, a cut there, and *voila*, Frederick's of DeKalb. I thought it was a costume ball *ala Mardi Gras*, so came as Medusa.

It wasn't a costume ball, but was fancy dress. Even so, the adders were a big hit. I had taken the precaution of having their poison sacs removed, but no one else knew that. They still could give you a good nip. Their fangs are like razors.

I had one hell of a time keeping them on my head for even a short while. I had superglued their tails together. That is one terrific glue. Well, they fell off right in the middle of the Blue Skirt Waltz and each of those snakes tried to take off in a different direction which resulted in a lot of hissing and biting of each other and anyone else that was near. Finally, six of them started off with a common goal, dragging a few resistors. They disappeared into the bell of a band member's tuba which got dropped in the melee. You can bet one musician is going to be in for a surprise when they drain the spit out of their instrument.

Everyone was pretty angry with me and I was so mortified that I fled the whole affair, losing one of my new slippers in the haste of my departure. I had such difficulty finding my size, too, size six triple E width. Almost perfect, perfectly round. My last pair I had bronzed and made into an umbrella stand. Perhaps some prince will find it and go off in search of the right umbrella.

Truly Yours,

Dear Sir,

Frieda, Gertie, and I closed the *Coughing Dog* the other night. We really had a blast. The happy hour just never seemed to end. We had fun reminiscing about our good old days when the trout just seemed to leap into the frying pan and there was a chick in every pot, yum yum. We had a special laugh thinking about our rodeo when you tied little Johnny unto the back of that young bull and it took off through the woods and all we ever found were bits of his clothes and blood stained trees. It seems like nowadays people don't know how to entertain themselves anymore. It all has to be done for them and then wrapped up in five pieces of plastic and spoon-fed to them with lots of sugar – with a liberal sprinkling of violence, extravagant special effects and loads of pulsating flesh. Then the whole kit and caboodle is so tightly wrapped up with enticing child proof caps that a lust-crazed gorilla couldn't open. Then it's all painted up with bright colors and shapes that will seduce and entice a child in such a way that the child will make that lust-crazed gorilla look like the Queen Mother herself at the most elegant tea party. Seems no matter where I start, I always end up talking about something completely different.

I read an article in the paper the other day about some lady who killed her husband of sixteen years and in order to dispose of the body she had cut the poor devil up and was charcoaling him. The police caught her as she was barbecuing his forearm. I found myself wondering whether or not she used the spit, what kind of charcoal she used and what type of seasonings. I guess

Grupp

we taste a lot like chicken. That babe at the other end of the bar at the *Coughing Dog* sure had a lot of white meat on her bones. ha ha. Keep in touch.

Truly Yours,

Dear Sir,

They decided that we had enough R & R, so its back to digging again and, again, the ground is dry and hard. We decided that if we could get a strong enough vacuum cleaner that didn't know when to stop sucking up dirt, we could plug that sucker in, not move it and go straight down to China. It sure would be easier on our poor backs. Course even if there was such a machine, we have lost all our electrical. We have not yet finished our wind generators but, when we do, we should have an abundance of power as the wind is relentless.

Everyone looks as if they have been sanded with a fine grit, because we have. It, the wind that is, has removed all sign of any paint off the northwest corners of all our buildings and frosted the glass on those sides as well. The dust sneaks in through every cranny and fills your pores right up to their tiny brims. You want to turn often, and also roll over in your sleep, so that you become evenly coated. One person didn't roll over all night and ended up listing to starboard all the next day. So now at night, we set our alarms to remind us to roll over every hour. It is like some scene out of a Max Sennett short.

Thank Heavens for the geysers. We built a structure around one of them and periodically steam ourselves clean. Sweating is the only way we could keep ourselves from becoming covered with clogged pores. I remember reading once that geysers exploded if you put detergent in them, I don't know if that is true or not. It certainly could make for a spectacular tour through Yellowstone National Park.

Truly Yours,

Dear Sir,

The wind has finally died down and we have all steamed ourselves squeaky clean. We all took turns flogging each other with birch branches; it sure gets the circulation into overdrive. Poor Douglas has had his prosthesis removed and replaced with a giant flyswatter, which has really come in handy for our saunas as well as the huge flying insect population that has been flourishing. With these huge insects come all sorts of diseases: malaria, sleeping sickness and itching welts. I have written a poem . . .

GENESIS Of
What, today, did the wise man say?
He talked of art and other things
and of the beauty to the world it brings.
But the greatest artist, he said
of all is one alive and working now,
a craftsman great of every tool.
Technique and material he does rule.
Who is this artist? What has he done?
The wise man said that everyone
and everything beneath the sun
and that and more are what he's done.
Where is this art? I want to see
that is as perfect as can be.
The wise man said, to one who sees,
he made the water-colored seas
and calmly carved the morning breeze
to stir his abstract sculptured trees.
He took a little lump of clay
and gently tore and broke away
and molded it into a shape.
And to this shape from lips did blow
a breath so pure that ,lo,

it caused the earthen shape to grow
to open eyes that once were clay.
He sent forth light that they may
view a work that's greater far
than any work of art before.
And from a mouth a silent tongue did wet
and turn to send a sound where none were heard.
The voice cried out that pity be
on the man who looks and does not see.

Truly Yours,

Dear Sir,

    I heard a story the other day about a little boy who
happened to be persistent, innovative and some kind
of musical savant. Anyway, his mother had bought him
one of those big gulp Slurpee's with a plastic top and
a straw. Amazed by the resonance of the sound he was
able to achieve while sucking up the dregs of his root
beer, the idea came to him that this large plastic cup
and cap and straw held the potential of a wonderful
sound. It took him a couple of years and about nine
hundred big gulps, but the cup became the bell of his

Grupp

horn and he finally found the correct place to insert the straw which he had cut and trimmed and punctured in mathematical increments. It became some kind of cross between a flute and a reed instrument. This young boy was afflicted with a bad harelip and protruding front teeth that presented his deformity to the world. His affliction that caused him so much social distress also gave him an unmatchable umberature so that, when he blew into this modified straw with his slender fingers playing over the puncture holes and with his other hand using the plastic cap as a mute, the whole musical scale plus some could be achieved. The tone of this instrument, I've heard, could cause Orpheus to weep with joy. The people that heard it said it could even heal small sores. He composed all of his own music that was unlike anything ever in the history of this Earth, unless Homer wasn't kidding us about the sirens. When his strange melodies were played, it made babies grin, women wet and cows give more milk. It wasn't very long before word spread and Carnegie Hall begged him for a concert which would have been terrific if on the way there he hadn't been run over and killed by a beer truck that was making a rush delivery to Madison Square Garden.

Truly Yours,

Dear Sir,

I apologize for not writing in such a long time. It really, really, really rained hard here this past week. It rained so hard that it just looked white outside. I was looking out of the patio door and the goldfish had escaped their pond and were staring me right in the eye. Then they went for a swim in the crab apple tree. I have never seen anything quite like it. I counted them the next day and somehow they had sense enough to get back to the pond before the deluge stopped. Some smart fish, eh.

We celebrated another wonderful Fourth of July with volleyball and Cajun chicken like Mama used to make with butter dripping corn on the cob, yummy yum.

The augers have been going day and night and we are working continuous shifts to attempt to make up for lost time due to all the rain. We are all quite exhausted, but everyone seems ecstatic with our progress. In fact. I have been spending most of my time sharpening the bits, which has been much nicer than being down digging in the shafts, as you well might imagine. Well, enough shop talk.

I heard on the news today that the Japanese are sinking more money into the study of bovine burping as evidently these ruminates belch up methane gas about fifty times per hour, which is challenging the strength of our fragile planet. Scientists from all over our planet are in a competitive mad rush to develop some kind of large Maalox pill that will soothe these poor beasts stomach's and save our planet from disaster. It seems to me that it might be better to capture this methane in little respirators that the cows could wear that we could then use to fuel our vehicles. Who would have ever thought that we could one day be dealing with cow power rather than horse power. *Understand you got a 260-cow-power engine in that baby, Roy,* doesn't seem to really have the right ring to it. Course, if you saw a stampede in one of those old cowboy movies you'd think differently.

Truly Yours,

Dear Sir,

You just wouldn't believe it, but the rains have started again, so much so that all digging has come to a soggy halt. The thunder and lightening have been terrifying and we have all been confined to our quarters. The small spaces and the rain on the metal roofs have been literally driving some of my compatriots over the brink. Fortunately, my colleagues' escape into insanity has been a diversion and wonderful source of entertainment for the rest of us. I, personally, don't really believe the rumors that any of them are homicidal. As I recall, the first one to snap was Ralph who woke up one morning reincarnated into Marlene Dietrich in the *Blue Angel.*

We all thought it was an act until we had heard him sing *Lili Marleen* about ten dozen times, all the while plucking hairs out of his legs until they were bloody. I should mention that Ralph resembles Marlene Dietrich as much as a Mack truck does. Which just seemed to make it all the more humorous to the rest of us: Ralph sitting on this stool, pants rolled up, singing in this husky voice *Lili Marleen* while he plucked and tore at the hair on his legs.

With all this, repetitive singing of German war songs caused a backlash with three other comrades going over the edge each believing themselves to be John Wayne, each one winning a different war. Marge became John Wayne the horse soldier leading some kind of cavalry attack on some poor Indians. She kept us awake with her constant galloping and trumpet TA tas. Roger became John Wayne the Green Beret who kept on calling in coordinates on our position. Andre ended up being the only John Wayne that was fighting the Germans, but in a very unlike John Wayne fashion, he really snapped and Ralph started to really look like Marlene Dietrich to him. Well to make a long story short, he tried to sexually molest Ralph which roused the guards and they were all taken away and our entertainment ended.

Truly Yours,

Dear Sir,

Everybody talks about the weather, but nobody does anything about it. I am, unfortunately, no exception. The rains have stopped, only to return us to this endless forty-mile-per-hour wind, which seems intent on flogging the wits out of us, if there are any left. Plus, we are now forging ahead into the dark days and so every day it gets colder and colder yet.

We have had no snow, yet. The holidays are sneaking up on us. Thank God, God had the decency to deliver us his son in the middle of this dreary time so we would have something to celebrate to take our minds off the cold. Just think, if Christ had been born on the Fourth of July. Firecrackers and Christmas trees don't mix, let alone the fire hazard of all that wrapping paper.

The spades and the picks have all been polished and sharpened, so I suppose I'll be returning to the shafts soon. The other crew has been lining them with wood to stop the cave-ins. It's interesting: the deeper we dig, the more it seems like we are going past past civilizations the same way an elevator in a fancy department store would go past Home Furnishings to Women's Lingerie, etc. Next stop, Jurassic, ha ha just kidding.

Douglas replaced his flyswatter prosthesis for a brace and bit the other day which he is most pleased with. The flies have all given up the ghost for this year. It reminds me of my friend who had a pit bull with a spinal injury. The dog was most ill tempered and would chew you up in a second,but loved my friend. And he LOVED his injured pit bull. So, he had a contraption made with wheels, aluminum and straps so that this beast retrieved its mobility. Can you envision it: snarling, foaming, large jaws snapping, wheels spinning, sparks flying? Its spinal injury didn't help its disposition one bit. Besides that, my friend had to massage his injured pit bull's legs in a hot bath nightly. With this injury, the dog also lost the muscle control of its bladder so he had to be taken outside every so often and have his bladder massaged until it relieved itself. I look towards a future with hopes that someone will do that for me.

Truly Yours,

Dear Sir,

Douglas has made his wishes known that he would like a screw driver attachment for Christmas. He has been having a ball with his brace and bit. Now that they have these new battery packs, Douglas's liability has turned into an asset, although he has not yet been able to solve his problems with personal hygiene and an electric screw driver has the potential of creating more damage than his hook. Was it Marshall McLuhan that talked about tools becoming extensions of our body? Douglas and the pit bull that I mentioned previously have become prime examples of McLuhan's theories. It is one thing to hold a tool, it is quite another to become the tool. With the aid of extra battery packs, Douglas has the potential of becoming the first living, breathing screwdriver. Which, if you know Douglas's mentality, can be quite terrifying. Not unlike giving a six-year-old one of those Israeli-made automatic rifles.

The weeks just seem to fly by; they say that is supposed to happen the older you get, but this is ridiculous.

I keep having this recurring dream where Judy Garland is having consensual sex with the tin man and they are using the scarecrow for a mattress . . . What does this mean? Judy doesn't have a stitch on, except for those ruby slippers. One of my colleagues here, who thinks he's so smart, has been doing all this reading on human sexuality. Just the other day, he says smugly "One out of every three farm kids has had sex with animals." So, I says "Oh yeah, well, one out of every three city kids has had sex with major appliances." That shut him up, all right. Another colleague then quipped "Well, now I know why I bought my refrigerator new." Perhaps this is what triggered my strange dreams.

Truly Yours,

Dear Sir,

The shafts are heaving in with the frost and Douglas is in his glory working with the team that is shoring them up. That screwdriver attachment has made him into a hero, as he can screw in the boards as fast as they can lift them into place. So, they are making great progress and are creating safer conditions for the rest of us. It's about time.

It's as cold as a well digger's ass and that is quite literally true and no joke. Speaking of a well digger's ass, I have discovered that since I have gained weight, my posterior has enlarged so much that, by manipulating my *gluteus maximus* muscles, I am able to pick up objects with it: towels, folded paper, and other small objects. It is almost like having a third hand. I can see with practice and exercise it might become quite a help. I wonder if this was a skill of early man that over the decades we have lost the use of. I read an article the other day about how they built the pyramids by mental telepathy, moving and vibrating these huge rocks into place via telekinesis. If you believe that one, using one's buttocks to carry your grocery list around is not out of line at all.

A few of us are going to *The Coughing Dog* tonight to help celebrate Lulu's birthday. It's hard to believe she is one hundred seven. She used to be state arm wrestling champ, all classes. She attributes her long life to once a week gin fizz enemas. She has lived a long time, but has been completely oblivious to everything for the past fifty years or so since she became addicted to this treatment. She hasn't been sick a day, though. In a moment of lucidity, Lulu giggled, "The germs just get pickled." We had a surprise party for her last year and she didn't even know it happened. The nice thing is we can all give her the same presents again.

Truly Yours,

Dear Sir,

The party at *The Coughing Dog* was a real blast. Frieda played the banjo and Gertie was on the pump organ and Yours Truly was on tambourine. Ralph was let out for the occasion, so he sang vocals. The whole crowd locked arms and started swaying back and forth to our music; it was very hypnotic. I should mention that Ralph only knows the lyrics to one song, *Lili Marleen*, whereas Frieda and Gertie have quite a repertoire of Stephen Foster favorites. You haven't heard anything until you've heard *Lili Marleen* sung to the tune of *That Daring Young Man On The Flying Trapeze*, or *My Old Kentucky Home*. Surprisingly, it didn't sound as bad as one might think. It infuriated Frieda and Gertrude, though, who are Stephen Foster purists. So they pulled out all the stops in their playing, in an attempt to drown

Ralph out. This, in turn, caused Ralph to sing all the louder. The place was really jumping. I don't understand how Lulu was able to sleep through it all. Occasionally she would wake up with a loud whoop and throw some change at Ralph or else attempt to stuff dollar bills into his pants, only to return face down to the table moments later. Well, this was all the encouragement Ralph needed and he really got into his singing. Can one sing a sad song to happy music? And who would win in such a conflict? Form versus content . . . Well, this night anyway, content won big. Ralph didn't so much sing as he sobbed the words. I didn't know that you could play a dirge on a banjo. But so contagious was Ralph's misery, it infected Gertie, Frieda and I so much that *My Old Kentucky Home* sounded like a Gregorian chant. Everyone was crying.

Things didn't lighten up until four people committed suicide. That kind of shocked everyone back to their senses. Ralph was led away to solitary, smiling with his success.

Truly Yours,

Dear Sir,

Well, here we are, another bitter cold day. It is so unbearable on the surface, that it is good to be down in the shafts, a fact I thought I would never admit. They are busy as beavers drilling some exploratory shafts to the west. The administration has decided to pipe in Muzak in hopes that we will be more productive. They say that chickens that listen to Mozart lay eggs with orange yolks and that, when cows are exposed to Bach, they give not only more milk, but it is sweeter and they are easier to milk. Muzak hath powers to soothe the savage beast, or is it breast. They have started out by playing us Frank Sinatra medleys which have so far not speeded up production, but have made us all incredibly horny – which makes one quite uncomfortable spending twelve hours a day toiling in the bowels of the Earth with other dirty, large, angry men. Even the canary we keep to detect poisonous gases keeps looking over its shoulder.

Speaking of the canary reminds me of the parakeet that my grandpa had that was bald as a cue ball. I don't know if it had ambitions to join a nudist colony or if it was infested with some kind of mites, but it only had a few feathers on its back that it was unable to reach to pluck out. It could have easily won an ugly bird contest, if there ever was such a thing. I recall that it used to sweat a lot, which might have had something to do with its condition. I wonder where the old saying "naked as a Jay Bird" comes from, as I've never seen one. My grandfather had taught it to speak in German. It's favorite saying was *comanzee here hound*, which it would

gutturally repeat over and over again as it would parade
. . . goose-stepping around it's cage. It's name was Otto
and it lived for quite a long time before it succumbed to
pneumonia. It's last words were *Gott in Himmel.*

Truly Yours,

Dear Sir,

We had a wonderful incident that involved a tortilla
the other day. There is a whole group of Mexicans that
work in the shafts with us. They usually eat in a group
away from the rest of us and they usually eat the same
thing: tortillas, beans, and a few hot chili peppers. We
have a small toaster oven that we can use to heat things
and they usually use it to heat their tortillas. Well, a
friend of mine was doing silk screens and he had a small
screen with a small image of Jesus's face on it. He got the
brilliant idea to silk screen this image onto their tortillas
with cooking oil. So one day he got his chance and did
this. Well, along came lunchtime and these fellas put
their tortillas into the toaster oven. The areas where the
cooking oil was became hotter and, slowly, up browned
a perfect image of Christ. As these poor devils saw this,

they quickly crossed themselves and fell to their knees in genuflection. They thought it was a miracle and were ready to erect a shrine . . . except our own howls of laughter and falling out of our own chairs alerted them to our fraudulent prank. Can you imagine the shrine, *Our Lady of Tortilla*, or something like that. Think of the possibilities involved in marketing: Christ-Endorsed Tacos, Jesus they're good. For penance this week eat five tacos and two enchiladas, umm umm good. Feed your body and soul at the same time. What does Christ look like anyway? Some say he's black. Some artists have depicted him with red hair. Some even argue that he was Norwegian.

Truly Yours,

Dear Sir,

    March has arrived like a lamb. What a blessing that is. I, for one, was really getting despondent over the cold and snow. I have been worried about frogs lately. It seems that they are disappearing from our planet. I remember when the highways used to get slick with them. I regret being so cruel to them when I was a child.

I tried to get me some as pets about fifteen years ago
at a bait shop and the man said he couldn't get frogs
anymore because there was a disease called Redleg that
was killing them off. Well, now they claim that it is the
crack in the ozone layer and too much ultraviolet light
is leaking through and damaging their eggs. Will frogs
go the way of the dodo bird? I certainly hope not. I find
myself thinking what frogs are the food source for ? ? ?
snakes, herons, elegant ladies in New York Cafes.

When I was a child I decided I wanted to taste
frogs legs and, so, captured a bucket-full of the largest
ones I could find and, like the great white hunter that
I thought I was, proceeded to execute them, gut them,
and dress them out. They fried up to almost nothing.
Now forty some years later, my heart fills with sadness
with the thought of them gone. They tasted a little like a
fishy peregrine falcon.

I heard a cardinal sing this morning and yesterday
ten thousand snow geese flew over, It was glorious. I
wonder if they eat frogs. Is this a warning sign to the rest
of us, like the canary in the coal mine? Or is it just part
of the great cycle of things?

Truly Yours,

Dear Sir,

Well we haven't had any rain in a long time now, watering restrictions are imposed. Every fifth person is allowed to flush the toilet so it gets rather rank, plus it has been almost impossible to tell just who is number five. This has been solved by having numbered cards hanging on a hook outside the bathroom. Some of my comrades have become terribly constipated in their attempts to just be number ones and several messy accidents have occurred.

In order to conserve on water, the kitchen has been making our oatmeal with orange juice which I have acquired a taste for. Sprinkle a little Tang on your cereal in the morning as a sugar substitute. No kidding, it's really yummy.

The temperature has bounced between ninety and thirty degrees, so we never know how to dress. That's one advantage of working down in the shafts as the temperature is consistent.

The social committee is trying to organize another party at *The Coughing Dog* since the last one was such a blast. The committee wants to have a theme. I have suggested the Revolutionary War, but we can't decide on which one. Douglas, who is working in the machine shop again, thinks that he could rig up a working cannon which would be fun.

In an attempt to bring culture to the outer limits, they have started up a poetry society. Every one has to write a poem to become a member. Here's mine:

There once was a girl from Japan
who fell in love with a young Chinese man
so she covered her ass
with pea pods and grass
and disguised herself as *moo goo gai pan.*
I was unanimously elected president.

Poetry sure is fun. Next we are going to start an art club, although a lot of the folks here are not good with numbers.

Truly Yours,

Dear Sir,

I am sorry that I have not written you in such a long time. The time just flies by whether you are having fun or not. Time seemed to stand still for me as a child, a minute could seem like an hour. Why is that? I've been told that as we grow older time speeds up . . . I wish it was the other way round. Perhaps as a child we are so anxious for some unaccountable reason to grow up. It's as if we are in some mad dash to solve the mysteries of life. The mad dash becomes so important to us that we miss life completely. Its like going on vacation or a trip.

. . our destination drives us onward and we miss the joy of the trip. In life, our final destination is death and its great question: *Then what?*

Grandpa said, "Heaven and hell are right here on Earth. It depends on what you make of it." Some children I see in films, however, don't have a chance to make anything of it. It's as if they are born into hell. It would be nice if we were all born with the same intelligence and the same opportunities, then one could feel a sense of pride in one's accomplishments, But as it is, any success or accomplishments have all been the blessings of fate or a higher power.

Is life a crap shoot or a roll of the dice? In our society now days, people take drugs to make them, for a moment, believe that they are something they are not, or alcohol to numb their senses because they feel too much. In our society, money is what is important. So, crime is rampant because people want things and they want them now. The goal is more important than how one gets there. Until the trip becomes more important than the destination, I can see no hope for our (ha ha ha) civilization.

Well, summer has come and gone again. The leaves are falling, but it has been unusually warm and humid today with a beautiful light. It is like living inside of a turtle bowl. So you can understand, with winter coming: I began this letter apologizing for it's lateness which is due to the fact that I have been quite busy watching the grass grow.

Truly Yours,

Grupp

Dear Sir,

Here we are again; it's finally come to this. I went and visited a beautiful place this past weekend, a waterfall in the woods fed by a narrow trout stream. The air was getting cold and there was a sprinkling of snow. At the top of the cataract, there was fluorescent green grass and moss with ice forming on it. I was surrounded by leafless white aspen trees and there was not one bird or a breath of wind, so it was silent except for the gurgling of the brook and the heaving of my own chest. Now back at camp lying in my own warm bed, I find myself wondering if it is still there and I feel a need to go back and check. To what end, I do not know. I guess, to just comfort myself, although as soon as I leave I would again still have the same feeling. I always want things to stay the same, yet I would quickly become bored, I think, if they did. The older I get, life becomes harder, more complex, more disturbing. It seems that in order to cope with life, one has to avoid life. How ironic a thought that is.

Nowadays, the world is small and getting smaller. It is a small wonder that my colleagues are stressed out and having strokes and heart attacks, for our society is going to hell in a handbasket via an overdose of drugs and alcohol and media gluttony. I see starving faces from across the world or people being tortured and slaughtered. I watch this nightly while I eat my supper, no wonder my digestion is affected. So we find ways of shutting things out, numbing ourselves to the cruelty and injustices of life so we can find sleep and peace. I find myself wondering why a man I don't know murdered a woman I don't know . . . . We are a curious people and our curiosity is so insidious and subtle that it is killing more than the cat. It attacks our very souls. Thank God for music and painting and all the arts that give us joy and release if only for a moment.

Truly Yours,

Dear Sir,

I can't believe it; since I last wrote you our good weather has continued to hold. Not that it makes that much of a difference; I am, again, working in the west shaft and it is a constant 60 degrees, which wouldn't be too bad if we didn't have to be in a stooped position all of the time. Some of my older comrades have their bodies stuck into a permanent s curve (because they have worked under these conditions for so long) with the added problems of banged heads and broken noses from their hard hats suddenly meeting the ceiling with great force and reacting true to Newton's Law producing a reaction of similar force on their nose. So there are a large number of old timers who in years are not old, but are bent over and breathe through their mouths because their noses have been broken over and over again. What this has done to their minds, I will never know, but suspect it has warped them as surely as these conditions have shaped their bodies.

Sometimes, the toll does become apparent when one of them goes over the edge and presents his other side to the rest of us, which is usually terrifying. A nightmare became real to us in the camp last week when Douglas, who as you may recall had his arm extended with that electric screwdriver, tried to play dentist with a fellow in the next bunk whose snoring was aggravating. I guess Douglas couldn't sleep with the high decibel snorts and wheezes that Roy was emitting and something snapped and he was on him like a starving spider on a juicy fat summer fly. Before we knew what was happening, Douglas did a root canal on Roy that you wouldn't believe. He had that screw driver revved up to full speed ahead when screams of "Eureka!" woke the rest of us. Douglas had hit what he took to be the mother lode, as this fellow had had a lot of gold inlays. Thank heavens that we came to our startled senses before we were all upon the poor wretch.

Truly Yours,

Dear Sir,

I read in the paper the other day about a man who accidentally stuck his car radio antenna up his nose and into his pituitary gland and lost a pint of blood but was expecting to be able to walk again in a week. Douglas had a similar problem when he attempted to trim his nostril hairs with his electric screwdriver attachment. Thank heavens he didn't hit his pituitary but took a sharp left into a sinus cavity, which he believes to be a great improvement.

Did you know that in the 1400's they used to slit horses nostrils? Yes it is true. I have seen drawings of them in books. They believed that the horse would be able to take in more oxygen and thus be able to run faster and have more stamina. Douglas does seem to be working harder and doesn't seem to get as tired as he used to. I am not thinking of doing that myself, however, nor do I wish to mention this horse story to Douglas as he would be after the rest of us and would be setting up a nostril-reaming clinic . . . and God knows where that drill has been. Douglas did take a large nick out of his nostril and didn't go to the infirmary to have it sewn up, so now it flaps when he breathes which can be quite distracting when you are talking to him about something serious or when he gets excited.

Truly Yours,

Dear Sir,

It has been too long since I have written, and where to begin. It seems it always begins with the weather. It is snowing outside. We have received around eight inches of light fluffy snow. It is like a fairyland, everything is so clean and pure, and still, and you seem to be the only thing alive and experiencing this beauty, whereas in the summer we are surrounded with life. You can see the plants grow if you sit still enough. Everything is transforming itself before your eyes, with the bugs, birds, worms, and flying things. Its hard, if not impossible to imagine it any other way.

Because of the cold, we are forced inside and into closer proximity with one another, which at times is difficult. As you are probably well aware, when large numbers of men share living quarters, flatulence does become a real problem. Well, a colleague of mine has developed a capsule that you take with your meals that takes care of the pungent odors, sweetens them, and he has developed a variety of fragrances so that when one expels gas it smells like cinnamon or vanilla or spring bouquet. He has even developed a new car odor. He is now putting all of his formidable expertise into controlling the pitch, resonance, and vibrato of this same flatulence and even has dreams of composing a symphony for flatulence. He has been creating these small reeds and whistles that, when fitted properly in one's sphincter, can duplicate the brass and percussion sections quite well. With high hopes

Truly Yours,

Dear Sir,

It has been so long since I last wrote. New loves have been made, and other loves have died. The glass always seems to be half empty or half full. Did you ever think about the words: *the last time?* What power these three words have for me

Europa and Friend   *color, lithograph*

Training the Pet   *lithograph*

Grupp   39

Fishing With Grandpa

We had to leave the river early and the fishing had been good, but my Grandpa wasn't done yet. So, as we drove home in an open topped touring car, he decided to begin fishing for birds. Over and over again, he would cast up into the sky. Casting and reeling in. Over and over again. Nightcrawlers for robins. Grasshoppers for bluejays and grubs for woodpeckers. But all he ever caught were a few sparrows.

Last Equestrian Portrait   *lithograph*

Grupp

Fantasy Bouquet II   *intaglio*

Grupp   43

The Summer of 1956

It was 1956, the summer before my senior year in high school. It was a time of hot Chevys, drive-in movies, Marlon Brando, Marilyn Monroe, James Dean and rock and roll. It was before Vietnam, Korea was not of concern to too many. It was Sioux Falls, South Dakota, in the middle of the country, a father-knows-best city of 60 thousand homogeneous inhabitants celebrating its Diamond Jubilee of 75 years. A Catholic-Protestant God-fearing haven where nothing was questioned and everyone affirmed each other. We felt we were without prejudice in this Norwegian / German enclave where there lived about 20 Blacks and a small Jewish population, no Hispanics, but one Chinese American restaurant.

Don and I worked at the Sunshine grocery store stocking shelves, sacking and carrying out groceries. In three years, I had worked myself up from 45 cents to a dollar an hour, the maximum you could make unless you learned to run the cash register. My needs were simple in those years, gas was around 30 cents a gallon and after work we would go to the A&W to antagonize the carhops by having them bring us out five nickel root beers each, which would require two trays and two trips. If we wanted: at Charlie's Pizza, 3.2 beer was available to us for a dime a glass or 75 cents a pitcher.

But tonight was special: it was Friday, the end of summer, and we had decided to go to the Sioux Empire Fair, which was just beyond the city limits and city laws and, because of that, could have, we had heard, a wonderful strip show. We had saved up some money for the occasion and had been planning this for the past three or so weeks. I had managed to tuck away eight dollars for this occasion; not easy, the way money burned holes in my pockets. So, Friday night at 9 o'clock, we hurried to mop the floors and closed down. We jumped into Don's 1950 black Ford and drove out by the quarry side of the fairgrounds where men with flashlights directed us through a maze of cars and potholes to a parking place in a big field of matted-down grass full of other cars. We ran and stumbled in the dark towards the lighted fair entrance like out-of-breath swimmers. A Shriner-type individual took our 50 cent admission at the gate and we walked into a world of mystery and magic.

After a short stop at the first corn dog stand we came to, we salved our appetites and continued our quest; munching away, dipping our corndogs into little paper catsup cups, we headed straight for the midway where they had the usual rides that made me sick and people threw dimes at Depression glass plates trying to win goldfish while others threw darts at balloons or softballs into baskets or at metal milk bottles. Even though barkers called us from every angle and we could see families carrying little Chinese food containers with goldfish and lovers walking with pandas or stuffed dogs, we were not dissuaded from our goal – although Don wanted to pitch the softballs into bushel baskets and it was all I could do to keep him on task and had to do some real fast talking as well as dragging.

I was afraid the place was going to close down before we got there. Everywhere we moved, we were tempted . . . THE HOUSE OF MIRRORS . . . THE TILT A WHIRL. A small tent almost caught us that proclaimed: SEE THE WORLD'S LARGEST RAT for only 50 cents, but I had to save my money. So, we finally made our way to the farthest corner of the midway our minds pummeled at every lobe. Slowly the lights and magic stopped and the fields began again. There it was, as I had hoped: the big tent.

GIRLS-GIRLS-GIRLS read the big, painted posters of huge-breasted, nearly-naked women. "Five beautiful girls and one ugly one," the unkempt barker with five o'clock shadow droned on in a southern drawl into a hand microphone. "Come on . . . . Come on . . . . two dollars for a trip to paradise." A woman dressed in only a pink, filmy robe paraded around next to him on the chest height stage while a speaker blared out *Rock Around The Clock* by Bill Haley and the Comets. Don and I looked at each other and grinned. SO FAR, SO GOOD.

I looked around to see if there was anyone I knew that might rat on me to my Dad. I'm sure Don did the same and then, as inconspicuously as possible, we each paid the two dollars and slipped through the canvas opening to a different world, the world of men, lots of men: farmers in bib overalls and caps advertising different seed and farm implements and West River ranchers in Stetsons. It took a while for my eyes to adjust to the dim light, the heavy canvas smell, and trapped cigarette smoke as everyone was either smoking or chewing.

As my eyes adjusted, I could eventually see that there were more of my classmates there but I didn't really know them – a group of tough kids from the other side of town. We acknowledged each other, but didn't share any small talk, although there was a sense of camaraderie in our being there. There were no chairs, just the rest of the stage you saw on the outside, chest high about eight by ten feet. We all bellied towards this where we could see well, but not too close so as not to be in any danger of being made to look foolish. The tough kids got in front of Don and me, which was OK with me. I could hear the barker attempting to get a few more people for the show. There was a speaker hanging on one of the tent poles that now played *Rock With Me, Henry* and other pop music.

I was eager for it to begin, and everyone seemed to get restless. FINALLY some red lights lit up the stage and we proceeded to wait again, kind of like waiting at the doctor's office and finally being called only to go to another room and wait some more. A few more stragglers came in and the barker gave up on the other side and reappeared through a slit in the canvas . . . and in a loud voice said "Here, directly from a successful tour in Kansas City, THE BEAUTIFUL

VERRRROOONICA!"

The music got louder and there was the same lady that we had seen on the outside. She spun onto the little stage, her long blond hair flying as she turned. She undid the ties on her pink transparent robe to reveal herself in all her cellulite glory in some kind of fancy bikini with a fringe on it that would accentuate her movements. The music got louder and raunchier as she whirled and undid the top of her bikini, which she twirled and then threw towards the slit in the curtain. She had a great pair of huge titties, each one magnificently capped with a small star and long gold tassel. Another twirl and she had dropped the bottom of her bikini. You still couldn't see anything, but it came damn close. A G-string with a larger gold tassel. She grabbed the large gold tassel and pretended she was jacking off with it. She turned around and spread her legs and that G string went so tight into the crack of her ass that you knew it must be there but you couldn't see it. I don't know how she did it, but she could make her butt cheeks shiver and shake in time to the music. I had only seen this a few times before in my life by horses making their flanks shake to get rid of flies. I was mesmerized. While she did this, she slowly bent forward at the waist until she looked at us upside down through her legs. I swore she winked at me. She stood up, turned around, kicked some switch on the stage, and the lights turned blue and she started moving in such a way that those tassels on her nipples started to go around clockwise. I don't know what she did next, but the next thing I knew they were going counter clockwise. She was great. Then, and I know you're not going to believe this, I wouldn't if I hadn't seen it with my own eyes, she had one tassel going clockwise and the other one going counter clockwise and she was working up a good sweat. At this time of my life, I would get a boner studying math, but Veronica had given me one that I thought would burst my pants. BOOM! She kicked another switch and the lights dimmed and the music stopped and that was the last I ever saw of Veronica.

Veronica was followed by a couple of older bored, tired strippers that caused some of the older men to get a big laugh out of hollaring, "Put it on! Put it on!" Finally, the barker strutted out like a scruffy rooster into the midst of the whistles and catcalls to announce that that was the end of the show . . . UNLESS you wanted to pay only two dollars more to attend their P.T.A. meeting, or should he say P.T. an A. where pasties and G-strings were a thing of the past. ALL WOULD BE REVEALED FOR ONLY TWO DOLLARS. There was a lot of grumbling and mumbling about a rip off, as men checked their wallets and tried to make up their minds. About a third of the farmers and ranchers decided they had seen enough. Don had too and started walking toward the exit. I said, " Cm'on Don, we've come this far; we can't quit now," with the urgency of a man climbing Mount Everest and having to turn back just before the summit. He relented. The barker collected our money and the other men without the vision or the resources had to begrudgingly leave. It got real quiet as we all jostled around for a good view of the stage. Our tough classmates had stayed and were now more comfortable and bolder and stood with their elbows on the stage.

The barker reappeared and said, "Now let's give a big hand for the star of our show . . . OOOOH MMMY – OOOOH MMMMMYYYYY – LOVELY TANGERINE . . . ." The lights went out, then pale pink and out stepped a girl with long red hair, not much older than myself in years anyway. The music got romantic sounding and she started a slow, seductive gyration around the stage. She was sucking on an orange popsicle and the juice was running down her body. She removed her robe and if she was wearing pasties on her young pink nipples, I couldn't see them. She would occasionally run the popsicle over her nipples and up the front of her green silk panties. She was pure, young, hot, raw sexuality. She would rub her crotch and, somehow, she peeled herself out of those panties and walked around the edge of the stage waving them in men's faces. As they grabbed for her, she would laugh and move away. She then lay down on that dirty stage bareass naked and writhed into different sexual positions in time to the music and really seemed to be enjoying herself. Then she sat up and scooted her way across the stage on her butt, over to Jerry, a tall wirey kid from my class whose goal in life was to be a rodeo rider. Jerry was wide-mouth gawking in the front row. I was afraid she was going to get slivers in her ass, but she was not new to this. As soon as she slid over to Jerry, she wrapped both of her long legs around his head and pulled his face into her crotch which he seemed to enjoy immensely and all the men were shouting words of encouragement. She bucked and moaned so, I thought she might smother him. Just when her screams and thrashing indicated she killed him, she disentangled her legs, rolled backwards, got up, and disappeared, leaving Jerry still alive and grinning from red ear to red ear as he gasped for breath. Jerry's entourage of friends surrounded him with congratulations. We were all stunned. I'm sure everybody in the place had a huge boner if they hadn't creamed their jeans. The extra two bucks had been worth every cent.

We were all blinded when a regular light came on over the stage and the Barker sauntered back out and held up a pair of dice. "These are not ordinary dice," he said, " but loaded dice and, if you shot craps with them, because of the way they are weighted and shaved on the corners that is unnoticeable to the human eye, they will come up seven or eleven each and every time." Why, just a few rolls and you would make back the cost of the dice. How could you go wrong? "NOT ONLY THAT . . . BUT THESE ARE VERY SPECIAL DICE! These are not just dots on the dice, but teeny tiny windows that you can look into when they are held up to the light." With that he held up a die and squinted into it. "Yes, men, from every hole you can hold it up to the light and see a nude woman in a different sexual position. And this other die is just like it except its a nude man ready for action . . . if you know what I mean. O.K. YOU'RE ahead of me, aren't you. With a strong light you hold both dice together like this and look through it and you have them in every position you can imagine . . . missionary . . . doggie style . . . 69. The entire Kama

Sutra of sex is captured in these dice and if you wiggle them like this you got some real action. These dice are so hot that we can't sell them to you, but we can give you a pair with this box of delicious salt-water taffy for only three dollars and fifty cents!"

Don and I looked at each other. "How much money you got?" I asked Don, regretting that I had spent a dollar on that corn dog. We calculated and pooled our resources and held up the money for the barker, who was now a comrade . They were selling like hotcakes, I was afraid that the guy would run out but he didn't.

The show was over, but we left laughing and happy, and I halfway expected to see Jerry's group of friends carry him off on their shoulders. I clutched our box of taffy as we made our way past the carney rides, back to Don's car in the field. I opened the box and found the dice and held them like they were the crown jewels.

"Quick turn the headlights on!" I said as I knelt down in the grass and squinted into a die at the headlamp. "I can't see shit," I said.

Don said, "Let me see." I watched hopefully as he squinted into the dice. "We were robbed!" Don exclaimed.

"Let's go to Charlies for a beer and maybe someone will burn a pizza." We were regulars there and sometimes; if a pizza got too burnt, they might give it to us or if someone left without eating all their pizza, we might beat the waitress to the leftovers. As we drank our beers, we rolled our dice on the bar in hopes that we might see a seven or eleven and the bartender probably wondered why I would occasionally squint and hold them up to the light.

The Circus is in Town   *ink and wash*

Exploding Still Life   *charcoal*

Grupp   55

The Sky is Falling   *pen and ink*

It Will Pass the Time *intaglio*

Grupp 57

Some Unanswered Questions
Pertaining to Polka Players

I have often wondered just where polka players come from. It seems like our young people cut their musical teeth on heavy metal or some equally rebellious noise that is aimed at causing their parents' and their parents' neighbors' fillings to loosen, if not from the decibels then from the gnashing.

Where then does this miraculous transformation take place? Is it on some road to Damascus where Saul becomes Paul or is our young Zeus tapped on the head and a full grown polka player springs forth, complete with accordion and liederhosen? Well, my questions led me on a mysterious odyssey where I discovered that there are secret Polka Camps hidden in the barren depths of central North Dakota. Children, mostly boys between potty training and kindergarten, are selected by roving polka scouts. They are then sold into Polka slavery via blackmail, bribery or whatever means necessary. These children are then raised in huge, underground sheds and will not see the light of day until fully mature or around 30 years old, whichever comes first.

The ceilings are low, so height is discouraged but width is not. They are raised by large-bosomed women who practice a daily regimen of pinching their cheeks so that, even though never exposed to sunlight, they take on a rosy, healthy look. They are force fed on a diet of dark lager, bratwurst, sauerkraut, and large quantities of tapioca. They are brainwashed into thinking day is night and night is day. They practice their accordions and their raucous shouting out of ooomp PA paaaa's. Basically, they will learn to live and breathe polkas until graduation, when they are finally blindfolded and taken away from the nest they have known and deposited in some trailer court in various parts of the Midwest and left to fend for themselves as best they can. Many fall by the wayside at this time, but some survive and even flourish. Thus this insidious cycle repeats.

sumi ink and wash

Fladmark Farm I

Grupp

sumi ink and wash

Fladmark Farm II

Grupp

lithograph

Dakota Road

64

Grupp

Great Piece of Turf

pen and ink

Grupp

Mexico

[Editor's Note: Carl Grupp, the prize-winning artist from Augustana College in Sioux Falls, SD, and Fred Klawiter, then a religious professor at the same school, set off in January of 1979, along with a vanload of students, for a month-long working-learning experience in Cuernevaca, Mexico. What follows is Carl Grupp's recollection of that trip.]

Across the Border

I saw a couple of vehicles detained where they were going through inspecting everything, clothes and stuff scattered all over the place. In our van, we had two top carriers that you had to sit on to close, holding all our suitcases full of clothes and necessities for our month-long sojourn. And so, I was afraid we could be detained here all day or longer, but we were blessed with a young, very pretty girl in our group who could speak Spanish. I could speak none and wasn't even too confident of my English. Thanks to her flirting, the border guard thought we were okay, peeled off a sticker, put it on the left inside corner of our windshield, and threw down the peeled off portion which quickly took its place along the chain link fence with the rest of the litter.

It was official: we were *turistas*, and off we drove to Monterrey. I was immediately struck by the poverty of the people on this side of the fence. Down the thin road we went with Fred driving and me with the map as navigator. The road was like what I remember of the highways in America in the 1950's, two-lane, basic asphalt except that the shoulders were lined with litter: broken glass, aluminum cans, and that wonderful 20th century edifice, used pampers. This view was occasionally dotted with dead dogs. I wondered if they became so starved they had committed suicide.

As we drove along, the land became more arid and desolate. Joshua trees sprung up like gigantic tarantula legs sticking out of the ground. Occasionally we would see the semblance of a lean-to made of a few sticks and, less occasionally, a person who lived at about the same economic level as a coyote, holding up a cage made of sticks tied together containing a lizard or a baby jaguar and some with hawks or falcons on their shoulders. The guidebook said that under no circumstances should we stop for one of these individuals. We never stopped, and the guidebook never said why we shouldn't, so I still wonder.

In Sioux Falls, South Dakota, a friend said it didn't matter where you ran out of gas as the hose would always reach. Here, the Pemex gas stations were few and far between in this seemingly desolate land. But we eventually came to one. While a young kid pumped gas, the students quickly evacuated the van to stretch and to use the restroom. To rate this restroom for hygiene on a scale of one to ten, this one would have received a minus twenty-four. It was enclosed, so it offered a modicum of privacy, which was both a blessing and a curse.

The kid who pumped the gas gestured that I hadn't paid him enough, although I swore I had. Fred who had also been an unbeaten Golden Gloves boxer grabbed the kid's hand that held the money and opened it up to reveal that he had folded a large peso note into his palm. We got our fuel and change and continued our journey, with me the wiser.

In some places, the road switched to three lanes, the middle lane for passing in either direction. If there was a speed limit, no one adhered to it and people were constantly playing high-speed musical chairs. When I was a child, there was an insurance company that put up big, diamond-shaped signs with a large X and the word "think," marking the exact spot where a person had been killed in a traffic accident. Well, in Mexico with its huge Catholic population, everywhere a person had been killed in a traffic accident, family members had built a shrine, some of which had little altars that contained burning candles. Some of these altars looked as though they marked the place where a busload of people had been wiped out, as the altars were overflowing with burning votive candles. I wondered who lit them in these desolate places.

I was driving now and was penned in by two large semi-trailer trucks belching black soot and the truck in front would occasionally signal a left turn, but would never turn. I learned that this was his signal that it was safe to pass. I think he was a practical joker, however, as

I would once have been met by a large semi, loaded with petrol and *peligrosa* signs all over it barreling towards me in the center lane. So I drove along with a good case of claustrophobia, sweating the idea of us becoming another shrine with fourteen votive candles. Besides the dead dogs and broken glass, you would occasionally see a burned-out semi truck on the side of the highway, the tassels and pompoms still hanging in the cab's window.

I was slowly learning Spanish. The students picked it up really fast. My knowledge consisted of saying "Gracias Amigos" a lot and a few swear words. I learned that *mirada* meant shit and, so, enjoyed shouting at the students, "OK who stepped in the *mirada*?" After driving past a lot of large smokestacks spouting flames – I soon discovered they were oil refineries – we came to a long, two-lane boulevard with leafless trees and railroad yards that announced our entrance to Monterrey, my first night in Mexico.

Our hotel was being fumigated, so they sent us to another place, where, up on top of the van we went to unload our suitcases for the night and then check into our rooms.

It had been a hard, tense drive, but Fred and I were hungry and eager to explore. I remember the stands with fruits and vegetables, how colorful they looked. We hadn't gone very far, when we came upon a man who was frying meat and tortillas on the top of couple of oil drums. In Bermuda, the metal would be stretched to make musical notes; here it was pounded into a concave frying pan. Fred and I looked at each other and the smell of the sizzling meat and said, "Let's go for it."

Borda Gardens   *color, watercolor*

I had heard horror stories of Montezuma's revenge, warnings not to drink the water, and tales of people who had screwed up their intestinal flora for months afterward. But Fred and I were both blessed with stomachs and appetites that agreed with Mexican cooking. We each gobbled six tacos, washed down with a huge, cheap Pepsi, all the while giving the chef our best compliments in English.

I loved walking around in the *zócalo* of whatever town we were in and buying the local food of the street vendors. I bought something from a little boy once that looked like a deep-fried cactus, he broke the crust with his fingernail and poured on some hot sauce from a goopy, encrusted bottle. The food was terrific and I never suffered any consequences.

The next morning we took off for San Luis Potosi, where we were able to park our van in a wall-enclosed

Cuernavaca   *color, watercolor*

parking lot and we were all adapting and beginning
to feel at home in our new country. As we traveled
southward we were like snakes shedding our skins.
Winter clothes were all packed away on top of the van,
the T-shirts were on, the windows were open wide
and, like bears coming to after a long sleep, we were all
smiling, joking and in great spirits.

In Cuernavaca

On the fourth day, we drove through Mexico City
into our destination of Cuernavaca and the monastery.
The monastery was situated on a hill out in the country
at least ten miles west of the city. The Benedictine
monks are noted for their hospitality and our living
quarters were their original ones. I had my own little,
sparse room with my own toilet, sink, and shower. A
single bed, desk, closet and one chair. A straw crucifix

finished my decor. The monks liked to be hosts, but also avoided people, so they had built their new quarters up higher on the hill.

My students and I spent a relaxing month painting in the Borda Gardens of Cuernavaca and the areas around the monastery. Here we painted in the land of the Aztecs, Cortés, the Emperor Maximilian and his wife Carlotta.

It seemed to rain every night and every day it was around seventy-five degrees to eighty – perfect. Not all the dogs were killed on the highways, as their sisters and brothers barked all night long. I relished the strange new smells and tastes of the markets, the warmth of the Mexican people, and their warm, healthy-looking brown skin. Every time I saw myself reflected in a mirror or a store window, I would think I was ill because of my Nordic/Germanic heritage bleached by the Dakota winters.

One day as I painted a fountain filled with large goldfish, a large purple-breasted turkey gobbled a short ways away and a great flutist on vacation serenaded us both with his beautiful music. The temperature was perfect, nothing in me ached, and my brush strokes went well. It was one of the most pleasant, peaceful times of my forty years.

The monks were great hosts and great cooks. In the mornings, they would kill and pluck the chickens that would be our supper that night. If, by chance, we didn't get full, there was always a basket of warm tortillas that we would lavishly spread with *cacahuate* [peanut butter] and the monks' homemade strawberry jam. You would always hear someone asking "Pass the *cacahuate*."

I was born and raised in the north central area of the United States, the youngest area of the United States in relation to European settlement. The people there were nomadic, so there is very little visual history, unlike the artistic heritage in Europe or in Mexico. Where I come from, art was looked upon as a frill rather than an important aspect of life. In Europe and now in Mexico, if I said I was an artist, I was addressed as "Maestro" and was held in high esteem.

We would spend the mornings and afternoons painting and the evenings were free time. I would sit under my top coat to paint since I am fair-skinned and can't take much sun. Another blond, fair-skinned student burnt the backs of his hands painting and would wrap them with toilet paper to protect himself. I was sitting under a shrub with my overcoat draped over my back to protect me from the sun, painting a large yellow canna lily, when I heard a gruff guttural voice: "Not bad!" I looked up to see a thin gentleman dressed in a white shirt, tie, and tan pants. Under a Panama straw hat, was the source of this voice: the hard, chiseled face of a man who knew he was always right.

"Hello, my name is Dr. Schneider. Maestro, why don't you come down and visit me, I'm an artist too," he growled. The next day was Saturday and I said that I would come and visit him after breakfast.

He lived right next to the monastery and I had done a painting of what turned out to be the back of his house a couple of days earlier. The next morning after a terrific breakfast of pancakes, I walked past the orchard out the gate and down the hill to Dr. Schneider's house. I walked down the sandy road past a small house of mud and tin that housed a family of five. The entire house was only about twelve-by-twenty feet. I saw many of these structures and always marveled at how that many people could live in such tight quarters; but the children always seemed clean and happy. A large pot of beans cooked over an open fire and the cactus and stunted shrubs held the brightly colored day's laundry scattered all over them. No need for clothespins, I thought, with the spines on those cacti. These women must clothes wash every day to keep their families clean.

I soon came to the large, wrought-iron gate that announced Dr. Schneider's home. I walked through and up a path and it was like the moment when the movie *The Wizard of Oz* turns to color. The contrast of

Dr. Snyder's House   *color, watercolor*

Dr. Snyder's Patio   *color, watercolor*

the wealth was incredible. The flowers were beautiful
and the entire place was lovingly manicured, compared
to the weeds and cactus on the other side of the
gate. Large sprinklers were irrigating the fields that
surrounded the house and people were working, taking
care of the banana plants. The house was brick and low
and long with a red tile roof and it sat behind a large
turquoise swimming pool. There was a covered veranda
where flowers of all shapes and colors were blooming,
Mozart drifted out from a large tape deck, large white
doves swooped all around, and small dogs played their
doggie games.

   Dr. Schneider and his wife were sitting on the
veranda. He was dressed the same, but was sitting at a
small TV table covered with a cascading small mountain

of notebooks and scraps of paper. Another TV table held a large, clear-glass ashtray filled with another mountain of ashes and butts. Directly across from him sat Mrs. Schneider who, despite the warm morning, had a shawl draped over her bony legs. Her hair was very fine and thinning, so she was wearing a cheap grayish-brown wig which was twisted almost sideways. It perched on her head like some small animal that had leaped up and clung there in fear for its life. A menthol cigarette dangled from the side of her thin, cramped mouth. Both she and her husband were drinking martinis, complete with olives, out of fine-stemmed crystal glasses. In her other fragile hand, she clutched one of those giant Hershey bars.

Dr. Schneider snapped, "Glad you could make it. Good Morning, Maestro. Would you like a martini? My girl makes the best martinis."

I replied, "Perhaps later." I was not accustomed to drinking martinis at nine o'clock in the morning.

He explained that he was writing his memoirs and that he had left Germany and had been a veterinarian in Canada and he used to vacation at the monastery and that he had become friends with the head monk, who had sold him the land. The head monk had been from Oregon and had been killed in an automobile accident the year before. (I wondered if we had seen his marker along our trip down.) He said the other monks disliked him and so now they lived in tolerance of one another.

The walls of the veranda were covered with Dr. Schneider's paintings. They looked as though they were painted by a deranged Soutine.

"I am painting the seven churches of Tepotzlan," Dr. Schneider said. "It is a little town near here. They have seven churches on seven hills. I think it's an important task." The paint was globbed on in slashing brush strokes.

"Very expressionistic," I said. The canvases were badly stretched and, so, warped and twisted out from the wall at strange angles. Seven exploding churches.

"Are you sure you wouldn't have a martini? My girl makes a great martini."

I relented and said I would have a beer. We sat down together and Mrs. Schneider said "I'm not supposed to eat chocolate, but I'm eighty years old; I can eat anything I damn well please. Would you have some chocolate?" She coughed as she thrashed away with all her eighty-year-old energy, attacking the candy bar's wrapper.

The beer and conversation went down easy and I soon gave in and let Dr. Schneider's maid mix me a martini. I sat sharing a large chocolate bar, drinking a martini, smoking a cigarette, and discussing the finer things of life as I watched their servants hoe around the banana plants. I got half crocked and excused myself and staggered out into their pasture to paint a watercolor of their house from a different view. It was one of the loosest watercolors I have ever done. It looked like nothing I had done before. It looked as if it had been painted by a deranged Soutine.

During our stay at the monastery, I was reminded of a colleague who had taken a group to Russia and had a student who fell in love with a Russian man and wouldn't come back to the states. After a lot of phone calls back to the college and her parents, he got her as far as Paris, but she refused to budge from there and he had to leave her. Well, we had a number of girls in our group who were enamored of some young Mexican doctors who would come and pick them up every night on their motorcycles. "God help me," I thought. "Don't let any of them fall in love or become pregnant while I am responsible for their welfare."

Racing Home

Our month in this Eden went by too quickly and I dreaded the drive back home. I longed to see my wife and children, but my hindside said, "I don't think I can take sitting that long in that van, no matter how nice

Santanias   *color, watercolor*

it is." We were packed in like sardines in our winter clothes on the way down, and we had all loaded up with treasures like blankets, sweaters, dresses, and other bulky items that would make our trip back more crowded.

We spent three days in Mexico City, visiting its museums, parks, opera house, the fantastic Museum of Anthropology, and the National Palace where I was bowled over by the Diego Rivera murals. Four out of every five cars were some kind of Volkswagen; I wished I had a dealership there. I was amazed that the VW's weren't all banged up by the amount of traffic.

On every telephone pole, you saw a poster of either the Pope, who was coming on a rare visit, or the actor John Travolta or Olivia Newton John. The big movie was *Grease* which in Mexican translated into *Vaselino*. We spent a day at the Aztec ruins of Teotihuacan, fighting off young boys selling obsidian flutes that they swore were played by Montezuma himself and onyx chess sets.

Then the mad dash home.

The trip back was going to be different, up the east coast in the Sierra Madres Occidental. When we left our posh hotel in downtown Mexico city at around six in the morning, a heavy fog of soot from the diesel trucks hung above us about seventy feet off the ground. The van was bursting with blankets and onyx chess sets. The students lay more than sat on their purchases that filled every square inch of the van. We drove past a high-walled building that was alone in the middle of a field, home to a leper colony. As we wound our way up and into the mountains, the land became more tropical.

Orange trees, lemons – a lush green land in contrast to what I had so far seen of Mexico.

What I didn't realize was that Fred is a closet Le Mans race driver. This became very clear to me as we tore around the mountain roads. We must have looked very much like a panel from a Donald Duck comic book where the car goes around the bend on two wheels while the other two hang out over the cliff. My right foot hurt from pushing down on the floorboards and my testicles were crowding my lungs. Fred persisted in driving despite my offers to drive. I was in the front on the passenger side and would look out and down and down at rivers that from our height looked like threads. On top of this, the roads were bad – no guard rails and in some places, due to a rockslide or a wash-out, our road turned into an iffy, hazardous one-lane. Fred would not relinquish the wheel, so there was nothing for me to do except look out and down and mutter prayers under my breath that God would guide Fred's hands on the wheel. So I just held on for dear life and took photographs out the front side window.

Occasionally, we would see people pulling or riding on large flat-bed carts, much like the carts that we had made as young boys out of discarded wagons, bicycle parts, and orange crates. These carts would be loaded down with bushel baskets overflowing with fresh-picked oranges, one person in front steering with a rope attached to each side of the front axle. Down the hill they would come like a bat out of Hades, with their board against a wheel for brakes.

We wound our way through seven different

temperature zones until we saw women walking along the side of the road with buckets of oranges balanced on their heads and the houses made of sticks with thatched roofs of banana fronds, much like what I had envisioned as the second little pig's home. I felt as though I was traveling through a National Geographic magazine and would not at all have been surprised to see bare-breasted native women appear.

We stopped at a wide place in the road to look down at a lush green, bountiful valley while two girls of our group disappeared into the bush to relieve their bursting bladders, only to be flushed out by a small group of men carrying curved sharp machetes. Thank God they meant no harm. The girls' sphincters probably closed up until they got back to South Dakota.

Thomas 'n' Charlie

The last rays of the day's sun were disappearing when we pulled into the small town of Tamazunchale. Fred parked in front of a large concrete slab about armpit height which acted as the outdoor patio of our destination, The Palacio Hotel. It felt good to stretch our legs. While Fred checked us in, I spied a small shop and went in. It was filled with birds and stuffed animals from the area. Large stuffed herons, egrets, reptiles and other beautiful birds. A complete bullfrog orchestra, large real green frogs stuffed and standing and playing tiny saxophones, frozen into the position of an eternal Charlie Parker. Frogs playing guitars, bass fiddles, etc. This was my kind of store, a kind of five-and-dime that would have made Alfred Hitchcock envious. I was very excited and purchased a stuffed Iguana for about five American dollars and a tiny hummingbird hanging on a thread. I hung the hummingbird from the Iguana's curled up tail and put it in the van on top of the inside motor housing.

I went into the Palacio just as Fred had gotten the keys to our rooms. The Palacio was as close to a palace as a decadent Tennessee Williams might imagine it through the lens of Elia Kazan. Fred's and my room was like a scene out of Casablanca, a sparse metal double bed with a khaki blanket that under no circumstances could cover your shoulders and feet at the same time – under a slowly twirling ceiling fan. Here we would eventually sleep like a scene out of a Laurel and Hardy movie. Fred was exhausted and told me then that he had driven so fast because a person did not want to be on that road at night. He was too tired to eat and just wanted to sleep.

The students meanwhile had congregated in one of their rooms to play a rousing game of cards. I, my appetite whetted from the strange store full of stuffed animals, decided to explore the town. It was getting dark and the little shop selling the stuffed birds and lizards was closed, but I could look in at the dirt floor which was still lit by a dim bulb hanging from a wire in the ceiling.

Directly across the street from the Palacio was a wide space in the road for a small bus depot where, I was soon to find out, large diesel buses stopped to refuel all night long. So, I later slept to the song of their gears grinding, motors revving, and their deep throat belches of black fumes. There was a small sign in Spanish where the macho bus drivers smoked and drank their coffee that translated to "Better Dead than Late." Before each driver returned to his position behind the steering wheel of his bus, he would cross himself and mutter under his breath. Now I realized more fully why Fred had driven so fast to get to Tamazunchale before dark.

The main street, as I remember, was only about six blocks long and consisted of warehouses loaded with oranges. Now I knew where those carts came from or went to. I felt no fear in this strange place because the Mexican people had been so gracious and good to me. The people had gone home and the town was quiet and dark except for the small bus depot and the Palacio. I wandered back down the deserted, dark street towards the dim light of The Palacio, disappointed in not finding any more places as interesting as the shop full of stuffed things. The Palacio had a small eating area inside and outside on the concrete raised patio. I stood looking at the glass case of candy bars, gum and lamps made out of cactus.

The Choctaw

It was here that I met him. He had dropped in for some gum or candy. He said "Hello, where are you from?"

I was surprised to hear someone speaking English. He had seen the Sanborn Insurance Card in my pocket that informed me how to translate dollars into pesos. I was five feet eleven and around two hundred pounds; he was a little smaller and about fifteen years older. A square kind face with a head of short-cropped, graying hair. He stood like a sailor steadying himself to the rotation of the Earth. I ordered coffee *negro* and he ordered warm milk and we sat down together at one of the Formica-topped tables, two fellow North Americans, a bond already joining us.

"What's happening back in the good ol' U.S.ofA.?" he drawled. I had not read a paper or watched a television set or listened to a radio for a month; no wonder I felt so peaceful. In America, we get ulcers and anxiety attacks from some horrible situation on the other side of the globe. I think about my mother for whom, as a child, the big news was who was going to win the basketball game: Mayville or Portland? Now, she worries about the crack in the ozone layer and how the rain forest in South America is being destroyed.

I told him about the weather on the way down and that the lettuce crop in the Rio Grande Valley had been wiped out. And that Muhammad Ali had regained his title from Spinks.

"Where are you from?" I enquired.

"I grew up on a Choctaw Indian reservation in Oklahoma," he said, "a good place for a kid to grow up, but a good place to get away from. The Korean War was going on and my friends and I wanted to be soldiers so we tried to enlist in the army, but we were not big enough and too young, so they wouldn't let us go and fight. So, we ate a load of bananas to get our weight up and lied about our age and joined the navy. We never saw combat," he said, "but when we got out of the service, strange occurrences began to happen."

One friend, he said, arrived home on the train and

his father picked him up at the station and, on the way home, the pickup they were driving was hit by the very same train and they were both killed instantly. Another friend went home and a week later they had a big party for his return and he got drunk and went up into the hills and committed *hara kiri*. His third friend arrived back home on the reservation safely and asked his parents about his horse. They replied that it was out in the pasture and had not been ridden since he had joined the navy. He replied, "That's not good. Horse should be rode." So he went out and lassoed his friend and put a saddle on him. But when he got on, he was wearing his navy slippers and his foot slid through the stirrup and the horse bolted and dragged and kicked him to death.

"So when I mustered out of the navy in Seattle," he said, "I bought a car and drove to the Oklahoma border, but couldn't cross the border. I pulled over and broke out into a cold sweat. I could not cross that border." His pale blue eyes stared into mine, "There is more to life than we can understand."

"So, I had saved all my money while I was in the service and went to Waco, Texas and bought a little gas station/restaurant and eventually married a Spanish woman who was from Tamasunchale. Every time she got pregnant, she went home to her mother – and we had nine kids so she and I spent a lot of time in Tamasunchale."

I told him I was an artist and a teacher. He said he had wanted to be an artist, too, but that it took a lot of courage to be an artist as people reacted to you funny, as if to show your sensitivity was some kind of moral

86 Grupp

weakness. He didn't get as good as quickly as he wanted, so he gave up the dream, but said his son could draw pretty well and asked if I would take a look at some of his drawings. Before I could answer, he was up and on the wall phone arguing with his sixteen year old boy about bringing his drawings down to the Palacio. I thanked God under my breath that the son won the argument.

"Maybe another time," he said as he sat down and ordered another warm milk and I got a refill on my coffee. Somehow the topic got around to Muhammad Ali, as it usually did with me. The great boxer was one of my heroes. My new friend and I shared our admiration for this American Icon. "Float like a butterfly, sting like a bee." My Waco friend said that Ali trained on a diet of rattlesnake meat and honeybee pollen and that he was on the same diet.

He said he was standing at a urinal a couple of years ago and his urine was the color of Coca-Cola. So he went to see a doctor at the Veterans' Hospital and they diagnosed him with bladder cancer. After a lot of tests the doctor said if he went into treatment in the vets' hospital that he might have about five years, but if he did nothing he might have a year.

"I decided a year in Tamazunchale beat five years in a veterans' hospital, so I sold the gas station and everything and moved to Tamazunchale." He was under treatment here by the town witch doctor and that's why he was on the diet of rattlesnake and honeybee pollen. He said he didn't want to get his hopes up too high, but since he had gone on this regimen his back aches had stopped and his urine had cleared up. He said he lived in a beautiful house just outside of town with a yard full of orange trees and flowers and every morning hummingbirds would fly in and out his bedroom window.

"Why don't you and your students stop for a visit in the morning?" he said.

I said I was sorry, but that I expected we would be in a rush to go back home.

"Well, if you can," he said disappointedly. He wiped the foam from his lips and continued, "Every town has a witch doctor and there is more than we can understand to Heaven and Earth. Whenever anything is wrong in the village, the people go to the witch doctor for consul. For example, take the man who owns this hotel," he gestured towards the man dozing near the cash register, "he is a man of habit. He has this pocket watch that he is very proud of and every day at a certain time he likes to take a shower and always hands his watch to his wife to care for. Well, one day he had done this and had gone off to take his shower when a whole busload of tourists pulled into town and they all came to the Palacio for filet mignons.

"The wife was not prepared for this and so took off her apron and put it on the table on the patio while she ran to the butcher to get the meat. She arrived back with the meat and had everything well in hand when her husband returned from his shower and asked for his watch back. The watch, which she always put in her apron pocket for safekeeping, was gone. So, that night when they could get away, they walked up the road to visit the witch doctor.

"Before they could say anything, the witch doctor said, 'I know what you have come for. You have come for your watch . . . but don't worry – all you have to do is wait. A little boy has taken it and he will return it to you.'

"So, the husband and wife went back home and, sure enough, a couple days later, into their hotel came a woman dragging a little boy by the ear. The little boy handed the watch back and apologized for taking it.

"There is more than we can understand in Heaven and Earth. A long time ago," he said, "I said to God, 'When you need me, call me, and when I need you, I'll call you, otherwise we will just leave each other alone.'

"I'm not afraid to die," he said, "but my wife is one of those Spanish women who mourn in black and I can't stand that. I told her when I die that she should have me cremated and to take my ashes up in a plane and to spill them over these beautiful hills and that she should have a great big party and go out and find a better man than I am.

"Come back in a year and see if I'm still here," he said to me. We got up and shook hands and I walked him outside where he got on a small motorcycle and put-putted up the hill into the darkness.

Magic Garden   *lithograph*

Grupp

What Come First? The Chicken or the Egg?   *color, color pencil*

The Sad Adventures of Mr. Toad

We had gone to Des Moines for a conference and went to visit their botanical garden which is in a geodesic dome. The inside echoed the outside in reverse and curved down to a lower pond full of beautiful koi. I asked the gardener where they got their fish as I had a small fish pond in my backyard with a waterfall that I had fashioned out of scavenged limestone, surrounded by ferns and staghorn sumac. Anyway, the gardener gave us directions and my friend, Lloyd, and I took off to find this pet store.

I was becoming enamored of a large, rare, blue goldfish while Lloyd came upon a cage full of large South African toads. They were huge, larger than any toads I had ever seen – each one about the size of two whopper burgers, yet they were on sale for five dollars each.

Lloyd decided he wanted to gift me one, as he could just see me taking my toad for a stroll down Phillips Avenue with a leash and harness. What an elegant image we would present to the neighborhood! At this point, I should mention that this was March – cold, too cold for strolling with an African toad.

The pet store owner had put my fish and toad in a large Styrofoam box, so that was the way they arrived at my home. My wife recoiled when we opened the box. I called my son, Carlie, to help me. My son has my name and I have the same name as my dad. Carl Grupps all, but when we were young, we were all Carlies. Well, we had an empty ten gallon aquarium that we could put him in, but what was going to keep him in there? Eureka! – a furnace filter with a two by four with books on it to hold it down.

"O.K. Carlie, when I put him in there, you be ready with the furnace filter and we will have him trapped." Once we accomplished this, we needed to create a good home for him. So, we added a bowl of water and some lettuce leaves.

The next day, I called the zoo to find out what he would eat. As I remember, they told me mealy worms or crickets. I called the local pet store and, yes, they had both, so I ran over there. The clerk asked me if I wanted regular hard-shell crickets or the imported soft-shell crickets. I replied that nothing was too good for my toad, so we would have the imported soft-shell crickets. He then asked if I had a cricket cage – he could sell me one. I replied thank you, but I will just use a paper bag. So he counted out a dozen, as that is how they sell them, and I quickly drove home to give my new pet a feast.

The three kids and I ran down into the basement with the sack of crickets. "O.K. Hold the top open and I will dump the sack of crickets in there and that toad will eat like a king." I got most of the crickets in there. The kids got the top back on and we all stood back to watch the carnage. Well, the crickets all jumped up on top of my toad's head and their feet were slipping and they were stepping on his eyes trying to get a good foothold. Some unfortunate crickets fell into the toad's water bowl and drowned. With the crickets stepping in the toad's eyes, he started thrashing around and tipped his water bowl over, spilling his water and drowning waterlogged crickets all over the bottom of the aquarium. I never saw him eat one cricket. Maybe he wasn't hungry or was bashful about being watched while he ate. So we left him alone. Days passed and occasionally I would go over and count the crickets, including their corpses that littered the bottom, to see if he had been feeding. Now, we included bits of potatoes as well as lettuce for the crickets to eat. Things went on like this for weeks until I noticed that one of the toad's toes was missing; he was cannibalizing himself. I called the zoo again but they were not interested in taking him. The weather warmed up and Carlie and I took him into the backyard. Carlie picked him up under his arms outside and he stretched out to about 18 inches and he took a huge leak, a stream that would have made a race horse proud. I think he had been holding it for fear of letting loose in his aquarium and drowning himself.

Finally, it turned into a nice day and the kids and I took him down to the river and released him. In seconds, he hunkered down in the mud on the banks and, if you didn't know he was there, you would not have seen him. We decided he would be the king of the Sioux River, said goodbye, and drove home.

Lost Horizon

Grupp

quill pen and ink

Another Riverscape

Grupp

97

The Magic Table

Grupp

sumi ink and wash

No Place Like Home

Grupp   99

Pig Head

I was teaching drawing, painting and printmaking at a Lutheran college in the middle of the country. I was asked to travel to a smaller community college about 60 miles away to do a drawing workshop, which I did. It lasted for several days and this college had a large, catered-in pig feed one night, so we all feasted on great pork and good dressing. The cooked pigs were carried in with apples in their mouths and olives in their eye sockets. As I got my plate of food, I asked if I could have the heads as I thought the skulls would be wonderful for my students to draw. The chef said, "Well, I'm selling hogs' heads over here," pointed . . . looked thoughtful, "Why not? I'll put them in a garbage bag for you." So as soon as I had finished eating, I picked up my bag of pig heads and put them in the trunk of my car and took off for home where I was going to meet my wife and good friend to watch a great boxing match on TV.

They were waiting for me. I said, "Come on out. You have to see what I've got." They did and I threw open the trunk and opened the bag, whereupon they both recoiled from the two pig heads staring at them.

The next day, I took the pig heads into my back yard

and started to try and clean the flesh off the skulls. I took my garden hose and with the best pressure I could muster, tried to literally blow their brains out. This attracted the curiosity of a little neighbor girl that had a beautiful bright-purple scooter she used to parade back and forth in front of our house. She did not even have to kick alongside as it had a foot pedal in the back that she would step on and it would propel her down the sidewalk.

She watched me with the garden hose and, every so often, asked "How are your pig heads, Mr. Grupp?" She kept track of my efforts as I soaked them in five gallon buckets of water and a dilute bleach solution (which I do not recommend as it turns the bones chalky). This went on for several weeks with Sarah asking me, curiouser and curiouser, "How are your pig heads, Mr. Grupp?"

Well, I finally got them quite clean and decided that it was time for the sun to do its work and bleach and dry them out. I had to put them some place where the dogs could not get them, so I brought out my ladder and put them up on my garage roof facing my neighbor's house. A couple of days later, Sarah came by and asked me about my pig heads. I told her that they were up on the roof, to which she replied, "They are not."

I said, "They are too."

She said, "I'll bet you they aren't."

I asked, "What do you want to bet, Sarah?" She then made a horrible mistake and said she would bet me her purple scooter.

I said, "O.K." and shook hands with her and walked

her out and around to where she could see the pig skulls up on the roof.

Her father called me later that night, asking for the return of the scooter and I replied, "You wouldn't want your child to be a welsher, would you?" So it now hangs in my garage alongside an old sled.

The Enchanted Window   *lithograph*

Still Life   *charcoal*

Grupp   105

Parable #V: The Prodigal Son   *intaglio*

Gilded Chicken   *color, lithograph*

Grupp   107

The Barranca

I had gone to Mexico, to the city of Jalapa, with 14 students of archeology and watercolor. We were hosted by an archaeologist, Mario Navarette of the Jalapa archeology museum . . . a terrific place full of those large Olmec heads. Anyway, he had told us about a small community at the bottom of this canyon, where he had encouraged the native women to start making ceramics as a way to get out of their poverty, and that some of these women were becoming quite successful at their craft. So we decided a trip there was in order.

Before I went to Mexico this time, I had my friend who is a gastroenterologist fix me up for the Tourista or Montezuma's Revenge. So, I had a whole arsenal of medicine for gastric problems, but had not planned on my back going out of whack . . . miserable in spite of well-laid preparations. Every morning, we would walk about ten long blocks downhill to the Los Amigos Restaurant for a bowl of soup made with some kind of fuel oil and, then, tortillas with *cacahuate* (peanut butter) which killed the taste of the soup, thank God. Once nourished, we would hike ten blocks uphill back to our hotel which made my back wrestle.

Shortly after one breakfast, we loaded onto a large bus for our trip to this town – and we would be some of the first tourists to visit this community, due to a new highway that had just been finished. So, like Lindy landing at Paris, we entered this community where people peeked out of their doorways at us and children raced our bus down the street, waving and cheering our entrance like conquering soldiers liberating their community. I should add that I am of Norwegian/German heritage, a redhead with very fair skin. I love the warm brown skin of the Mexican people and was always surprised and shocked to witness myself in a mirror as I would think I was sick or anemic. Well, one of the kids surrounding our bus was a redhead who really, really looked at me like I was a lost relative. My heart went out to him.

Our bus was too large to go into the canyon, so Mario dealt with a large, beefy Mexican fellow who had a dump truck and would be willing to take us down into the *barranca* and bring us back. It was decided that the students would ride in the back of the truck and, since my back was out, I would ride in the cab of the truck with the driver. Now, there was a wealthy non-traditional student taking archeology who was about my age, a slim, good-looking woman dressed like she was on a safari: leopard-skin skirt and jacket and a sun hat with tie-down silk, straight out of the wardrobe of Katherine Hepburn in *African Queen*. She decided she wanted to ride in the cab. Since she jumped into the cab before me, she squeezed in between the driver and I. I should mention that this truck had a floor shift and the driver and I were each over two hundred pounds, so it was a snug fit for (I will call her) Teddy's perfumed body. All settled in, we took off on our quest to visit one particular lady potter.

It was a beautiful day and could not have been improved upon, unless my back was feeling better. We were heading down the good highway back to where we came from. I could see the canyon off to the left. When, Geesus Kuriiiist, the driver took a hard left towards the canyon. Was this guy a suicidal maniac? No. There was an unseen, by me, single-lane, gravel road heading to a road that was carved out of the side of the gorge. Down we went; I was looking out over the edge straight into the canyon. This road was just barely one lane and I worried about us meeting anybody, plus it was crude and rocky, which jolted the truck this way and that as we rumbled down its treacherous path. We went along this way, me praying under my breath that our driver was stable.

We eventually came to a level area and stopped where workers were harvesting sugar cane: men and mules loaded down with sugar cane, coming together at a gasoline-powered, giant, metal wringer that the workers were feeding the sugar cane into. The juice was being squeezed out into a wooden trough with gas jets underneath it where it was cooking and boiling in a large dark room.

The men carried their meager lunches in plastic buckets and were generously eager to share with us. Their lunch consisted of tortillas with a few beans and perhaps a radish or two. I thought mine was wonderful as I hadn't eaten since breakfast. They had another bucket, full of what I assume was home made rum, that we all took sips from. After this nice little interlude, we all loaded back into our truck and traveled toward a small community of mud brick houses and occasional corrugated metal roofs. When you looked up out of the top of this canyon you could see huge power lines and a cable that came down to power the town. The driver took us to the center of town and said we should be ready to go after a couple of hours. A man was walking down the street toward us, carrying a large turkey with a purple breast.

Mario took us to this lady's home. She was about four and one half feet tall and about three feet wide. She welcomed us into her home. One wall in a room had a homemade shrine. Beautiful lace doilies were draped everywhere and on each one was carefully placed votive candles that were burning. Reproductions of Jesus and various saints decorated the wall centered around a large straw cross. There was a wire hanging from the ceiling with a single light bulb that illuminated this space. The floor was packed, hard dirt; chickens and small pigs walked through the house occasionally while we were there, like this was the usual state of affairs.

The students and I crowded into a small space to watch this woman work her magic. She took out her tools for ceramic work, which consisted of a small disk of wood that she would build her pot on, an old corncob with no corn on it, the leather tongue from a shoe, and some smooth stones for polishing the clay. She got on her haunches and started making a pinch pot, pinching the clay she had into coils, all the time turning the wooden disk that she was building her pot on, at the same time shooing the chickens away. Some of her pots were huge. I could fit inside one of them. In this simple manner, she would create ceramic wonders.

Outside there was a makeshift kiln where these women would fire their pots, fueled by any animal dung that they could find.

Well, the time was soon up and we had to load back into the truck for our trek back out of the canyon while the light was still good. Teddy jumped into the cab again before me and nestled in between the driver and me. I think the driver might have been waiting for us in a small bar, as I suspected that he might have been drinking. With the students all loaded in the back of the truck, we took off to drive out of the canyon.

Everything went fine the first part of our trip, until we stopped at a small house near where the people were harvesting the sugar cane and we all got out and had some more of their homemade rum. I suspect that this house had a way of knowing whether a vehicle was coming down the narrow road along the side of the gorge. After a few sips, we all returned to our places in the truck and the driver took us up the narrow trail that had so terrified me on the way down. As we bumped along on this narrow road, all of a sudden Teddy's finger nails sunk into my arm and she whispered to me, "Just keep talking Carl." The perfume and the proximity had become too much for our driver and he had fallen in love with Teddy. I glanced over to see the driver's hand slide off the gear shift to Teddy's nyloned thigh, creeping towards the Promised Land. Oh my God, he wasn't looking at the road, but was trying to make contact with Teddy. I looked up at the rearview mirror where I could see the lower part of the driver's face, which was making kissing motions towards her. She slapped his hand and said "Stop it, you rascal" . . . I was thinking, don't do anything that would disturb his control of this vehicle and send us over the precipice. I envisioned our bodies mangled and tangled together at the bottom of the canyon with the driver's hand still locked onto Teddy's thigh and us a small blurb in the local paper back home.

The driver, who was now oblivious to the fact that he was driving this vehicle along the edge of a huge cliff and was mesmerized by his own lust and Teddy's perfume, then grabbed the gear shift and jammed the truck into low gear right between Teddy's long legs. She squirmed against me and I leaned as far to the right as I could, saying, "God, Teddy, don't do anything that will make his hand jerk on the steering wheel." This scene repeated itself a couple of more times before we came up to the main highway and headed back towards the town and our large bus.

The driver drove past our bus, however, and took another road up higher, Teddy asked me, "Where is he taking us?" I suggested to Teddy that she might be payment for our trip. Teddy found my humor lacking, however. The driver took us to a big bluff that looked out on an amazing view of the town and valley that the driver wanted us to see. Afterward, we loaded back into his truck and returned to our large bus, bid sad *adieu* to the red-haired boy, the dump truck, and headed back to Jalapa.

Iris Waltz   *lithograph*

Grupp

Still Life Bouquet   *pen and ink*

Grupp   117

Squirrels and the Lone Ranger

When I came to teach drawing, painting and printmaking in a small college in the middle of the United States, little did I know that I had to build the room that I would teach in. The building was a one story barracks salvaged from the Second World War put to new use as the college cafeteria. It was now being resurrected as the new art department. The kitchen area would become the printmaking workshop. The chair of the department had a space walled off into a new office for me. This was very nice, but they forgot one thing . . . heat. In the winter, I taught wearing overshoes and a coat and scavenged a milk-room heater used for the nude models to heat my office as well. When I was given this space, I went to work with a broom shovel and paintbrush. For three months, a lot of the faculty thought that I was a custodian rather than the new art teacher.

Well, I had gone to work one day and grabbed a chuck roast bone that still had quite a bit of meat on it and put it in a plastic bag for my lunch. At noon, I went into my little office to have lunch. I sat down on the floor to get closer to the space heater, wearing an olive green top coat as well as my overshoes. I had a tiny transistor radio that required small batteries to run. I turned that on and dialed it in until I got an old radio transcription of the original Lone Ranger show. I should add here that I grew up with radio and every night my family would gather around the supper table and listen to the Lone Ranger while we ate our supper. So I was in seventh heaven. I took the bone out of its plastic bag, salted it and proceeded to gnaw the meat off. Tonto had just nursed the Lone Ranger back to health after the Texas Rangers had been ambushed by the Butch Cavendish gang. They had all been killed except for one.

Tonto said, "Kimosabe, you are the only one left. You are now . . . LONE RANGER." Tonto buried them all and made an extra marker so it would appear that the gang had killed the Lone Ranger, too. They rode off tracking the Cavendish gang with Tonto and the Lone Ranger riding double as the Lone Ranger's horse had been killed by the gang. They came up over a rise and saw a white stallion locked in a death battle with a large buffalo, the bison was just coming in for the kill when the lone ranger shot the bison. They camped and nursed the injured horse back to health.

Tonto said, "Are you going to keep him, Kimosabe?"

"No, Tonto. He's too magnificent an animal; I have to let him go."

As the horse walked away, Tonto said "Hmmmm, look like silver in sunlight."

"Yes, that would be a good name for him, Tonto. Look! He's turning around. He's coming back. Here, Silver, UP BIG FELLOW!" I burst into tears.

At that moment there was a knock on my door and I was brought back to reality. I opened my door and saw Connie, one of my students. I forgot to add that this building was infested with squirrels and a baby squirrel had fallen through a hole in the ceiling in the design room. I said that all the students should take a break for a bit and maybe the mother who was looking out the hole and chattering (I assumed directions) to its baby, would come down and collect her stunned child. That worked.

Not too long after that, I was acting chairman of the department and decided we should have a candy machine in the building. So, I called a candy company and they agreed to install one. This started out as a fine idea, but as I came into the building and on the way to my office, I would pick up shredded candy wrappers and think, "The students sure are getting messy. We need a garbage can near the machine." But, even with that, every day there would be more wrappers on the floor. I had never bought any candy, but the company would come out once a month collect their money and refill the machine. Well, when they did this there was very little money, but most of the candy was gone and the tray that caught the candy when it would drop down was full of squirrel feces, so the company packed up the machine and left without a word. We decided that we had diabetic squirrels, as they ate the chocolate-covered cherries but left the granola and the salted nut rolls.

The Magic Omelet II   *lithograph*

Dakota Bouquet II   *lithograph*

Grupp   123

Ode to a Caterpillar

From when
From what
From which
Or were
Comes a worm with legs
And fuzzy fur

intaglio triptych

Diogenes' Dream

Diogenes' Dream

The story of **DIOGENE'S DREAM** began when I had returned from a month-long interim in Cuernavaca Mexico. I had gone to an all-college faculty meeting where I sat and doodled and tried to feign interest. I did a loose drawing of a clown sitting and drawing on a pad. Little did I know what that would become.

That night, I went to my basement studio and decided to do an etching of this idea. I had a copper plate previously covered with hard ground [*an asphalt-like substance (asphaltum) placed on the copper – artists draw in the ground, scraping it away with a needle, then place the ground-covered copper plate in acid where all exposed regions of the plate are eaten away and will hold ink, becoming lines on paper once the ground is cleaned from the plate, ink is smushed into the lines, and paper is pressed against the plate*] and began loosely drawing the seated clown. I thought, "What is he drawing?" and decided to have him drawing a nude model. I was drawing with a steel needle through the thin ground beside a small jar of the asphaltum ground that I can paint on over mistakes (*On the finished piece, this will leave a light scratch on the copper – as opposed to the deeper*

Changing   *intaglio*

Grupp

lines produced by the acid bath, which I enjoy as it leaves a memory of my thought process). As I drew my mind wandered and I began thinking about the seven virtues and vices, a great theme in the history of art. So I began to clothe my nude model and turn her into the figure of Justice complete with scales and blindfold.

At this point, my whole concept changed to the virtues and vices. So I looked around the studio and, as luck would have it, I had put hard ground on two more copper plates of the same size. I had a 4 by 8 foot piece of plywood that I fashioned into a larger drawing table, rigged so that it was on a slope, where I could put these plates on next to each other. Each plate was 18 by 24 inches, so combined they became an image 24 inches high by 54 inches wide. I put a strip of wood on the bottom for the plates to rest on, I then began to draw on the plates standing up, not defining anything because I did not yet know what was going on, so I just worked with rhythms of loose circular marks, and like Newton's law that every action should have an equal but opposite reaction. I worked like this very loosely until I felt satisfied enough to begin. I then sat down and, like da Vinci, looked at my marks as a child looks at clouds and let the drawing talk to me. On the ground next to Blind Justice, I began to draw a seated figure who turned into the Greek cynic philosopher Diogenes who, as you may recall, spent his life searching for an honest man. So here he sits with his lantern next to him tearing out his hair. Behind him, another loose circle became my youngest daughter holding a doll. She represents Hope and the future. Behind her walks a church bishop praying

The Human Condition *intaglio*

with his eyes shut and next to him is a military general wearing dark glasses so neither can see where they are going. The ground by the feet of Justice is littered with human skulls that, to me, symbolize memories. To the left of Blind Justice's head is a self portrait in the background, whereas to the right of her head, people whisper to her. Death wears a top hat and between her and the artist clown scholar sits a black Labrador dog. Right behind Justice is the tree of knowledge rising up to dead branches and on a clothesline hangs a white sheet to accent the artist clown scholar and make him the main focal point of the piece. This central panel of this work is titled **CHANGING**.

THE HUMAN CONDITION is the first panel to the left of changing. You see the foot soldier and Death following the general and priest, and in front of them is an old lady holding a baby, signifying birth and death. Behind her is the juggler attempting to keep all the balls in the air and behind him flutter flags of patriotism and gaiety. A nude Bacchus sits cross-legged on the ground, symbolizing Gluttony and Sloth. To his left, comes a crippled man on crutches, while behind him is the Grim Reaper with his scythe. A man lies on the ground, being cared for by a woman. This represents sickness and charity or wanting to be mothered. Immediately behind her a man carrying a child walks out of the flames. Almost unseen, lies a sleeping Labrador signifying the sleep of reason. Behind the sick man sits the mad fool astride a crouching skeleton. He clutches a broken hourglass and all the sand is falling out. To the left of the mad fool, anchoring the left side of this triptych,

Illusions   *intaglio*

Grupp

stands Adam in front of the ladder to the tight rope that turns into a clothes line. Balloons create false gaiety while the perch on the pole echoes the mortar board hat of the artist clown scholar. Out of flames are menacing clouds, yet we see the left side of the rainbow rising over the dead tree of knowledge and connecting the triptych.

ILLUSIONS: In the left side of the third panel, we see the figure of Vanity looking into a hand mirror and holding a cut flower. Below her sits a large vase of flowers. Kneeling on the ground is another clown attempting to coax a turtle coming out of the ocean to jump through a hoop. This is the symbol of Patience. Behind him is the mad fool just looking on, while up above on the tight rope walks Faith, but he is going to be tripped up by two love birds that are perched back to back, one looking up at Faith and the other looking down at Eve who stands and anchors the right side like an exclamation mark. I had etched a large curtain behind her to make it more like a stage set, thinking all the world is a stage and we are but the players in it. I decided against the curtain and scraped and burnished it out. I put in a geometric grid behind these figures to counter the organic flow of the figures and to also create the illusion of a stage set. The triptych contains earth, air, fire, and water. It goes from night to day, war to peace. The ground is rocky on the left and smoothes out to the sea and plants grow behind Eve.

Each print is a complete composition and can stand independently. Anyway, when I named it, I felt that the human condition is changing illusions. So each print has its own title, but when they are all joined together.

. . . My lifetime partner Carol Wright suggested I call it
Diogenes' Dream, so I did.

While I was working on the plates, my students
would ask me what it was about. I would reply, "My
friend who suffered with being manic depressive and the
changes that I had witnessed in the Catholic Church in
Mexico." Which was what I really thought at the time.
My students would nod and think I was full of prunes.
I slowly came to realize that it was about the destruction
of my marriage of 16 years, which had blindsided me,
but subconsciously I must have felt it. When one works
from their imagination, I have discovered it allows one
to speak from deep within. A priest would occasionally
come in and watch my progress, He was also an amateur
psychologist who said he was glad that I had removed
the curtain and that the tightrope continued on as
that meant that I was moving into a new life. I have
continued on, learning from others' observations. For
example, the white sheet turns the tightrope into a
clothes line and becomes a symbol of surrender. Or as
another suggested, innocence. Or as another suggested,
that Grupp was just hanging out all his dirty laundry for
others to see. Another person looked at patience holding
the hoop and asked "Why is this figure holding a ring?"
. . . so it becomes the proposal denied.

Nine of Birds   *color, lithograph*

Genesis 2:31   *lithograph*

Grupp

The Divorced Man's Cookbook
and Household Tips

When my wife of 16 years divorced me, she took the stove, the refrigerator, the freezer, the washer and dryer. When I asked her how come she took all of these necessities, her answer was she needed them. But, she left me the fondue pot and figured that was fair.

I am a large fat man with a gruff voice. I picked for my attorney an old high school classmate who was a large fat man with a gruff voice. His back was bothering him, so he would lie on the floor of his office while interviewing me. He asked how many of my wife's friends were divorced. I answered, "Most of them." He said, "Oh, that is not good; in the land of the divorced they sit upon the other side and beckon them over unknowingly." I thought, this is not a gruff man; he is a poet. The one thing that my attorney did to protect me was to give me first option to buy the house back, which I did because I hoped things could be like they were. I eventually purchased a used gas stove from a lazy home ec high school cooking class and found a Maytag washer that was sitting on the curb for sale for 100 dollars. I still use it 28 years later.

Anyway, I had my three kids over for fondue and started thinking of writing my own cookbook. To begin, there are four basic food groups: CAFFEINE, NICOTINE, ALCOHOL, and CAMPBELL'S CREAM OF MUSHROOM SOUP. It would also include some household hints like: a piece of string or thread wrapped around ones fingers makes a great cheese slicer. Who needs a vacuum cleaner, when a good leaf blower does double duty?

One of my favorite recipes is my meat loaf which is best in the winter. I use one pound of Italian pork sausage and one pound of ground buffalo which is very lean. To this, I cut up and add one green pepper and one large yellow onion and one box of cheap stuffing mix or pulverized crackers. I then add cream of mushroom soup and one small can of mushroom bits, one cut up jalapeño pepper and one or two eggs. I will also add onion soup powder or taco seasoning if I have them. I smush them together really well until the phone rings. I will then squeeze them into meat loaf pans and frost them like a cake with refried beans. It is delicious and I will eat off of it for a week.

The cookbook will also contain practical, cautionary tales for the newly bachelored. For example, my oven does double duty as the hideout for my cooking kettles and celebrated popcorn pot. So, I have to take everything out and set it on top of the stove. I set the oven to 350, then the cat and I go into the living room for an hour to watch the evening news and prepare for the feast.

The first time I baked this, while we were waiting, we were both alarmed by what sounded like a bomb going off in the kitchen. It is a small kitchen and pots and pans were thrown all over the place with such force that it was lucky neither the cat nor I had been in there as we could have been killed. The walls were dripping with oil and oregano. After much consternation and befuddlement, I realized my stove has a heat vent in the top and back where all sorts of heat blasted out onto a can of Pam which then rocketed upwards like a missile and indented a solid plaster ceiling at least a half inch deep. As if that weren't enough destruction, it blew the hell out of my bargain glass jar of oregano . . . which explained the walls. I started to wipe down the place and sweep up the broken glass.

Thank God the meat loaf was in the oven and protected from the blast and was therefore edible.

Fable of the Gold Fish and Grapes

Grupp

When in Doubt, Punt

Grupp

143

Waiting for the Muse   *color, watercolor*

Melancholia   *pen and ink*

Grupp   145

The Trap

I didn't think a thing when I found my drain cover off. I figured I had probably kicked it at some time while doing laundry. They are supposed to screw on, but mine is an old house, built around 1910, so my cover just sits there. My dog is now old and sleeps a lot, but once a day Bessie comes alive like a puppy and gobbles her food and rolls on her back and, sometimes, when I feel energetic, I chase her from the dining room to the living room to the hall to the kitchen and back to the dining room again, her toenails spinning on the hardwood floors and the kitchen linoleum.

I should tell you that I am a bachelor by way of divorce. Everything I touch seems to turn to clutter. I shove things aside on my kitchen countertops to prepare my meals and my dishes hardly ever see the inside of cupboards, going from the drain sink via the fry pan into the dining room where I scoop out a place to eat at a table that would comfortably seat six for an elegant meal. Please don't get the impression that I am dirty, no, just cluttered.

Like a lot of Americans of our time, I am inundated with junk mail and everything I buy is wrapped three times. My dog and I produce enough garbage and waste to make any sanitary engineer lick his chops. Anyway, my dog Bessie likes these burgers that come in ten or twelve cellophane-wrapped packages inside a box, a treat that I alternate with canned dog food to augment her dry dog food. Bessie is spoiled. I had noticed that one of these burger packages was open and leaking burger bits out into the lower cupboard shelf where I kept it along with my sugar, flour and cereal. Well, my lady friend, Carol, has a dog, a pup, a lovable little mutt and he and Bessie seem to tolerate each other. His name is Woodrow – anyway I just thought Woodrow had gotten into the burger bags.

I cleaned up the small mess and thought little of it, until a few days later when I found the same conditions, but Woodrow hadn't been for a visit.

My basement is as cluttered as the rest of my house. Boxes, lumber, half-full paint cans decorate the walls and build up in the corners. I thought I noticed movement out of my peripheral vision, but blamed it on my bifocals.

It was the fall of the year and my old friend Jerry had flown out from California for his annual visit. Jerry and I have been friends for close to forty years. We share, besides our history, a lot of the same interests: art, music, literature, and movies. Anyhow, when Jerry visits, we usually stay up late and eat great volumes of popcorn. Jerry grabs the remote and flips from channel to channel in a quest for an old Oscar Levant movie. Oscar didn't make too many movies and has been dead for a long time, so the surfing of the channels is an endless and futile search.

It was around one in the morning and Jerry and I were eating popcorn and Jerry was surfing the cable channels when I heard a noise in the kitchen cupboard and realized that I must have mice invading my gentle domicile. I found some traps and baited them with chunk style Jiffy peanut butter and cleared a spot for them in the shelf next to the dog burgers. "This will do the trick," I said. Jerry nodded and flipped the channels with vengeance.

The next morning it was a Saturday so I didn't have to go to work but got up early and went downstairs with the expectation that Santa, perhaps, had come during the night. I opened the cupboard door to witness my success, but found one trap had been sprung and the other trap was completely missing. Where the hell did it go? This was no ordinary mouse, but the king of all mice. Not only that, but the place was trashed. Whatever it was, I had made it quite angry and it had vented itself on my towel drawer, throwing everything every which way.

I went to the hardware store after breakfast and purchased a rat trap identical to a mouse trap but four times larger. This one had a formidable spring on it and I was exceedingly careful when I generously spread Jiffy on the trigger mechanism and pulled the spring back and set it. I cleaned out a larger space in the cupboard so that nothing would hinder the strength of its arc. Now there was nothing to do but wait.

That evening, would you believe it, *Humoresque* was on channel 53, an old black and white John Garfield movie where Oscar had a big part. It was an omen, the tide was turning in my direction. As we watched *Humoresque* and munched on popcorn, I expected to hear a large snap and screams from my kitchen, but it was as silent as a tomb. I wanted to check my trap, but forced myself not to peek and perhaps let my quarry know my plans. I am not a hunter, but I was thrilled by the chase and anticipation of capturing my quarry, this cursed interloper that had intruded and violated my home.

The next morning, I awoke and hurried down the stairs to see what I had caught. I opened the cupboard door to find the trap twisted and bent and the dog food and dish towels scattered all over. This was indeed a very formidable mouse. Sorry, I could not help myself. I lied. I opened the cupboard door to find a large grey and white rat with its head in my rat trap. I carefully carried it out to the garbage can, pulled the wire up and dropped it in. It was over a foot long, not counting the tail. If a fish, it would be a keeper.

When I came home from work, and I'm not sure why, I went directly to the garbage can to check on my trophy. It was there but had moved. Was it still alive? It was now standing up as if trying to escape the can. I came into the house and told Jerry that I thought it might still be alive.

We went out for supper to the grocery store salad bar and when we got home I ran out to see the rat again. It was in a different position than it had been in before. It didn't look a bit alive, but was in a different position.

Stunned, I kept mentioning it until Jerry, annoyed, admitted sneaking out and moving its corpse in the garbage can to fool me. I believe him.

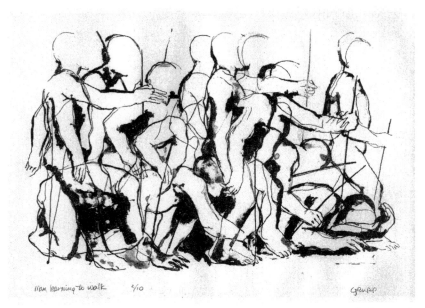

Man Learning to Walk   *lithograph*

Third Person Bouquet   *color, color pencil*

Grupp   153

Fortunes Told   *pen and ink*

Weird Opera   *color, mixed media*

Grupp   155

It Just Wasn't Her Day

I was wandering the gift shop at the old Walker Art Center, when I spied a rubber fish for three dollars. Little did I know the joy this rubber fish would bring me. I need to digress a little bit: I was a college professor and tried to look the part (long hair and a full beard and I had purchased a brown corduroy sport coat with leather patches sewn on the elbows).

My coat had two inside breast pockets, in one I kept my checkbook and in the other one I carried my new rubber fish. When paying for my groceries at my local market, I pulled out my checkbook and accidentally pulled out the rubber fish so, with great flourish, I juggled it around like it was still wriggling and then attempted to write with it before asking the clerk, "Do you have a pen? This fish won't write."

A couple of weeks or so later, my friend and I were driving to Chicago to see an art show. We were someplace in Wisconsin when we decided to take a break at a café. We went in and sat down. A nice, old, blue-haired lady came over to take our order. I told her I would like a piece of apple pie with ice cream, a cup of black coffee and a glass of water for my fish.

I went to use the rest room and came back in time to see our waitress put down our orders. She said she was so nervous, not having worked for 30 years, but her husband had passed away and she needed more income. She said she had already dropped some dishes and had spilled milk on one customer. She hoped the pie and ice cream were to my liking and did we need anything else?

She left and I took my rubber fish out of my coat pocket and placed it face down in my water glass so the tail was sticking out. With my peripheral vision, I could see our waitress staring at the water glass with the fish in it. She disappeared back into the kitchen and I took the fish out of the water glass, dried it out with my napkin and returned it to my pocket. At this point she stepped from the kitchen with the cook, the dish washer and another waitress, all staring at my table. I heard her saying, ". . . but, but he really had a fish in his water glass." I guess it just wasn't her day.

People are no Damn Good   *color, ink and watercolor*

The Horrible Snoose Brothers   *color, ink and watercolor*

Grupp   161

Modern Living   *lithograph*

Fiddler on the Roof   *lithograph*

Grupp   163

Carol and I In Edam

About a year and a half after my divorce, I met Carol and we started dating. We were both art instructors and it was coming up on the 100 year anniversary of Van Gogh's death; Amsterdam was planning a huge exhibition of my hero's work. Carol and I spent many evenings looking at maps and saving our money to make the trip to see a show of 300 of Vincent's paintings in the new Van Gogh museum in Amsterdam and then another 300 of his drawings in the Kroller Moller museum in Otterloo. This story is about the start of this trip.

We flew out of Logan in Boston for Amsterdam and it was a long flight, I am a nervous flyer. We arrived in Amsterdam at nine the next morning, exhausted but excited. Carol was feeling ill. I rented a car, a nice small Buick, and asked the clerk if he knew of some place out of the city we could stay. He made a phone call and confirmed a place in the Hotel de Fortuna in the small city of Edam, about 20 miles outside of Amsterdam. He drew out directions for me and I signed the papers and, with Carol as navigator, we took off, driving through the industrial part of Amsterdam, eager to find Edam.

As we drove along, the landscape became more rural with pastures of cows and sheep. I did not see any pigs, however. We drove alongside canals and you had to cross bridges to leave the road.

We eventually came to the sign for Edam, turned off the highway and pulled back into the 16th century. It was wonderful. We drove into the town and I said, "Now, how are we going to find the hotel?" Immediately, Carol announced, "There it is." We were right by it, so we parked the car and walked over to the Hotel Fortuna which was made out of old, adjoining buildings. We walked into a room of varnished wood covered with a rich brocade. It was like a sumptuous Vermeer except with platters of sliced ham, hard-boiled eggs, fruits and vegetables: a table set for Dutch masters like Van Huysum or deHeem.

The lady in charge was waiting for us and checked us in. She said that all of the rooms in the hotel proper were booked so she would give us a room out back. We walked outside by the side canal into a lovely garden of tuberous begonias, an orgasm of reds, yellows, oranges, whites and pinks. Little fountains trickled and birds in cages sang to welcome us to this Eden.

There were two buildings out back that were, at one time, stables. We walked into the darkness of the first building and were directed up some steep steps to the second floor. We were shown the bathroom and she opened the door to what would be our room and she opened the large Dutch windows that looked down on the garden. The double bed had an orange coverlet with a black and white kitten curled up in the middle of it. It was all too perfect, like a wonderful dream. The lady that booked us in said that we were the only guests in this building. Told us the rules of the hotel, when breakfast was served, and gave us our keys.

She had dyed her hair and had plucked her eyebrows and so was able to paint them on with the mood for the day. Today, I felt she was feeling quizzically benevolent. Everything was so perfect, except for one thing I could not put my finger on for a while. Eventually, I realized that everything was so perfect, like we had gone back in time, except for one thing I noticed which seemed so out of place when we moved into our lodging. It was a vacuum cleaner by the steps to the second floor.

We went out for a bite to eat and a walk along the dikes of the Zuider Zee. I celebrated by buying a beer, the first one I had had in months. We sat out at a table behind our building that was along the back canal and looked across at an old boat works. A duck begged bits of bread from us.

Carol was exhausted and nursing a bad cold so we retired to our room. Carol collapsed into the bed; I was feeling amorous but Carol was having none of it. I tried to be good and laid down and tried to sleep. I shut my eyes, only to see our landlady looking at me. Whereupon, I asked her, "This is all so lovely; where did we screw it up?" She took a long deep breath, arched her eyebrows and said to me in all seriousness, "Electricity: that's the curse what done it." I thought about it, agreed and started laughing hysterically. When I laugh it is not a chuckle but a torrent of loud guffaws that caused the bed to rock and the walls to shake. This disturbed Carol who screamed at me, "Get out! Get out . . . go down the hall to another room. I have come to Europe with a lunatic!"

Chastised, I went down the hallway to another room, sat down and attempted to sober up, although I only had one beer which must have been teaming up with jet lag. Here I was, in this beautiful place, with this beautiful blond in my bed, and a voice within me saying, "Carl, don't screw it up." I smoked a couple of cigarettes until I thought I was O.K. and attempted to sneak back into bed beside Carol. I shut my eyes, and there she was again, looking down at me saying, "Lectricity: that's the curse what done it," which set me off to giggling again, biting on my fingers to stop it.

Lost View of Mount Fuji   *lithograph*

Grupp

Succulent Bouquet   *charcoal*

Grupp   171

Generic Newsletter of Carl Grupp
1999

Well, here we are again. I suppose the biggest change in my life this past year has been my finding a stray young cat living in my garage. It would go in and out a broken window. This was early last spring and it was quite cold out. One day, I felt sorry for it and decided to give it some food. As far as I knew, all cats ate were saucers of milk and fish. I had neither, but had some old gooey ice cream in the back of my freezer, so I put some in a dish and brought it out to the garage.

The cat would hide in a pile of lumber which I had slowly collected. Whenever I came near, it would peek out at me. I should preface this with informing you that I am a dog person who has measured out my life in Black Labradors and have never had much time for cats; just as when I was a child we fell into two camps: Gene Autry or Roy Rogers (I was a Gene Autry devotee). Later on, we fell into two camps: Ford or Chevy. I believed the Chevy to be far superior. I have always felt a little bit of disdain and superiority over cat lovers.

I called Carol and told her that I was attempting to make friends with this stray cat in my garage and informed her about the glob of ice cream. She told me that cats were carnivores and liked meat. I said, "O.K."

She then asked me what I had named this creature. I had not thought this far, but blurted out, "FIDO." Carol said you couldn't name a cat "Fido." I quickly replied "Yes I can. Fido is his name."

She then asked me if it was a boy or a girl, I replied, "I don't know."

"Since it's a cat," she rebounded, "you have to spell it P-h-y-d-o."

I said, "Well, it's a Cajun cat."

"In that case," Carol said, "you have to spell it P-h-y-d-e-a-u-x."

I hung up the phone and ran to the grocery store for some cat food, a part of the store I had never ventured into before, and bought a small plastic container of soft and moist, chicken and liver flavor, which seemed to appeal to me. I drove back home and poured some on top of the ice cream goo. And sat back and watched Phydo feast.

This went on this way for several weeks. I added a cardboard box with a blanket in it so she would be warmer in the garage as it was still quite cold out. Well, I found this miserable creature occupying more of my thoughts and would always fill the bowl with food and check to see if I would see her. Then I made my first major mistake.

I was sitting on my deck, enjoying a cup of coffee and a smoke and had left the side garage door open. She came out and over to me and wanted me to hold her. Which I did. Then came the major mistake. I said, "Do you want to see where I live?" and gave her a tour of my home, not unlike a realtor. She walked behind me as if she was asking about the copper plumbing and how old the wiring was and could she sharpen her claws on that leather chair. After the tour, we returned to the deck and her to the garage.

I jumped in the car and returned to that mysterious place in the store in search of a litter box and litter. When I returned home, she was waiting for me on the deck and followed me into the house as I set up the litter box by the stove in the kitchen. She knew it was for her and had probably been saving up, as she immediately took a dump in it. She stayed in the house that night and ever since. I have had her fixed and spent a small fortune on inoculating her against every known cat disease. I found out from the vet she is a she.

This all doesn't sound too bad, and it wasn't at first. Times were happy, it was summer and warm and I would leave the door open for her to run in and out and play. An old friend was over and we were listening to music and talking when, suddenly, I became aware of quite a ruckus in my kitchen. I got up to look, and there was Phydo disemboweling a bird in the middle of the room. The bird was still alive, yet was being ripped to shreds, and the air was thick with feathers. I managed to chase Phydo through the house and out the backdoor, leaving behind a trail of fine, floating down. It was horrible. This was not a sparrow either; no, it was a mourning dove, which I love.

I should tell you that I have spent years planting plants that will attract birds, supplied them with a heated water dish in the winter time and have bird houses and bird feeding stations all over my small back yard. And then I introduced a cat into this haven. Word has gotten out and now my place is barren of my feathered friends.

I never had Phydo declawed and the back of the leather chair I now sit at to type this is a testament to their razor-like sharpness. I'm glad it is winter and the windows are closed as, in the summertime, my neighbors hear me screaming, "Come here you little shit!" or "Get out of there you little shit!" or "Get off that you devious little shit!" Phydo thinks that I have changed her name to "Lil Shit" as that better suits her.

I am learning patience and feel I must be doing some kind of weird penance for some character flaw in my relationship with this obstreperous beast. I don't have it in my heart to banish her back to the garage, yet I struggle with her feline ways. Please pray for me, that I may find peace with this nasty varmint and please remind me that she is one of God's creatures. If I appear to be a little stressed on my Happy New Year cards, it has something to do with her ceaseless, annoying meowing that occurs when I am sleeping or drawing or for that matter all sorts of inopportune times.

Nevertheless, I wish you and yours a very joyful and happy entrance into a new century.

Davey Crockett   *pen and ink*

Untitled   *photograph*

Grupp

Interior font is Adobe Garamond Pro.
Exterior font is Arial.

Made in the USA
Charleston, SC
19 December 2014